"Caw, caw, caw, caw, caw!" yelled Blacky at the top of his voice.

FRONTISPIECE. *See page* 132.

BURGESS TRADE QUADDIES MARK

MOTHER WEST WIND "HOW" STORIES

BY

THORNTON W. BURGESS

Illustrations by
HARRISON CADY

GROSSET & DUNLAP
PUBLISHERS NEW YORK

By arrangement with Little, Brown, and Company

ISBN: 0-448-02766-6 (TRADE EDITION)
ISBN: 0-448-13730-5 (LIBRARY EDITION)

BY ARRANGEMENT WITH LITTLE, BROWN, AND COMPANY
PRINTED IN THE UNITED STATES OF AMERICA

To the cause of conservation of wild life and to increase of love for our little friends of the Green Forest and the Green Meadows through awakened interest in them and a better understanding of their value to us as faithful workers in carrying out the plans of wise Old Mother Nature, this little book is dedicated.

CONTENTS

LIST OF ILLUSTRATIONS

I

HOW OLD KING EAGLE WON HIS WHITE HEAD

PETER RABBIT sat on the edge of the dear Old Briar-patch, staring up into the sky with his head tipped back until it made his neck ache. Way, way up in the sky was a black speck sailing across the snowy white face of a cloud. It didn't seem possible that it could be alive way up there. But it was. Peter knew that it was, and he knew who it was. It was King Eagle. By and by it disappeared over towards the Great Mountain.

Peter rubbed the back of his neck, which ached because he had tipped his head back so long. Then he gave a little sigh.

"I wonder what it seems like to be able to fly like that," said he out loud, a way he sometimes has.

"Are you envious?" asked a voice so close to him that Peter jumped. There was Sammy Jay sitting in a little tree just over his head.

"No!" snapped Peter, for it made him a wee bit cross to be so startled. "No, I'm not envious, Sammy Jay. I'm not envious of any bird. The ground is good enough for me. I was just wondering, that's all."

"Have you ever seen King Eagle close to?" asked Sammy.

"Once," replied Peter. "Once he came down to the Green Meadows and sat in that lone tree over there, and I was squatting in a bunch of grass quite near and could see him very plainly. He is big and fierce-looking, but he looks his name, every inch a king. I've wondered a good many times since how it happens that he has a white head."

"Because," replied Sammy, "he is just what he looks to be,—king of the birds,—and that white head is the sign of his royalty given his great-great-ever-so-great-grandfather by Old Mother Nature, way back in the beginning of things."

Peter's eyes sparkled. "Tell me about it, Sammy," he begged. "Tell me about it, and I won't quarrel with you any more."

"All right, Peter. I'll tell you the story, because it will do you good to hear it. I supposed everybody knew it. All birds do. That is why we all look up to King Eagle," replied Sammy.

"Way back in the beginning of things, old King Bear ruled in the Green Forest, as you know. That is, he ruled the animals and all the little people who lived on the ground, but he didn't rule the birds. You see the birds were not willing to be ruled over by an animal. They wanted one of their own kind. So they refused to have old King Bear as their king and went to Old Mother Nature to ask her to appoint a king of the air. Now Mr. Eagle was one of the biggest and strongest and most respected of all the birds of the air. There were some, like Mr. Goose and Mr. Swan, who were bigger, but they spent most of their time on the water or the earth, and they had no great claws or hooked beak to command respect as did Mr. Eagle. So Old Mother Nature made Mr. Eagle king of the air, and as was quite right and proper, all the birds hastened to pay him homage.

"So King Eagle ruled the air and none dared to cross him or to disobey him. Unlike old King Bear, he accepted no tribute from his subjects but hunted for himself, and instead of growing fat and lazy, as did old King Bear, he grew stronger of wing and feared no one and nothing. Now this was in the days when the world was young, and Old Mother Nature was very busy trying to make the world a good place to live in, so she had very little time to look after the birds and the animals. Thus she left matters very much to King Eagle and old King Bear. They settled all the quarrels between their subjects, and for a while everything went smoothly.

"King Eagle made his home on the cliff of a mountain, so that he could look down on all below and see what was going on. Every day he went down to the Green Forest and sat on the tallest tree while he listened to the complaints of the other birds and settled their disputes, and none questioned his decisions. Now after a while, this little part of the earth where the animals and the birds first lived became overcrowded. It became harder and harder to get enough to eat. Quarrels became more frequent, until King Eagle had little time for anything but straightening out these troubles and trying to keep peace.

"Old Mother Nature had been away a long time trying to make other parts of the world fit to live in. No one knew when she was coming back or just where she was. King Eagle, sitting on the edge of the cliff on the mountain, thought it all over. Old Mother Nature ought to know how things were. He would send a messenger to try to find her. So the next day he called all the birds together and asked who would go out into the unknown Great World to look for Old Mother Nature and take a message to her.

"No one offered. This one had a family to look after. That one was not feeling well. Another had a pain in his wings. One and all they had an excuse until Hummer, the tiniest of all the birds, was reached. He darted into the air before King Eagle. 'I'll go,' said he.

"All the others laughed. The very idea of such a tiny fellow going out to dare the dangers of the unknown Great World seemed to them so absurd that they just had to laugh. But King Eagle didn't laugh. He thanked Hummer and told him that his heart was as big as his body was small, but that he would not send him out into the Great World, for he would go himself. He had been but trying out his subjects, and he had found but one who was worthy, and that one was the smallest of them all. Then King Eagle said things that made all the other birds hang their heads for shame and want to sneak out of sight.

"After that, he told them that no king who was worthy to be king would ask his subjects to do what he would not do himself, and that where there was danger to be faced or something hard to do, it was the king's place to do it, so he himself was going out into the unknown Great World to find Mother Nature and see what could be done to make things better and happier for them. Then he spread his great wings and sailed away, every inch a king.

They watched him until he was a speck in the sky, and finally he disappeared altogether.

"Day after day they watched for him to come back, but there was no sign of him; they began to shake their heads and openly talk of choosing a new king. Only little Mr. Hummer kept his faith and day after day flew away in the direction old King Eagle had gone, hoping to meet him coming back. At last a day was set to choose a new king. That morning, as soon as it was light enough to see, little Mr. Hummer darted away, and his heart was heavy. He would take no part in choosing a new king. He would go until he found King Eagle or until something happened to him. Pretty soon he saw a speck way up against a cloud, a speck no bigger than himself. It grew bigger and bigger, and at last he knew that it was

King Eagle himself. Little Mr. Hummer turned and flew as he never had flown before. He wanted to get back before a new king was chosen, so that King Eagle might never know that his subjects had lost faith in him.

"He was so out of breath when he reached the other birds that he couldn't say a word for a few minutes. Then he told them that King Eagle was coming. The other birds had proved that they were not brave when they had refused to go out in search of Old Mother Nature, and now they proved it again. Instead of waiting to give King Eagle a royal welcome, they hurried away, one after another. They were afraid to meet him, because in their hearts they knew that they had done a cowardly thing in deciding to choose a new king. So when King Eagle, weary and with torn wings and broken tail feathers, dropped down to the tall tree in the Green Forest, there was none to give him greeting save little Mr. Hummer.

"King Eagle said nothing about the failure of the other birds to give him greeting but at once sent little Mr. Hummer around to tell all the others that far away he had found Old Mother Nature preparing a new land for them, and that when she gave the word, he would lead them to it. Then King Eagle flew to his home on the cliff of the mountain, and not one word did he ever say of his terrible journey, of how he had gone hungry, had been beaten by storms, and had suffered from cold and weariness, yet never once had turned back.

"But when Old Mother Nature came later and announced that the new land was ready for the birds, she first called them together and told them all that

King Eagle had suffered, and how he had proved himself a royal king. As a reward she promised that his family should be rulers over the birds forever, and as a sign that this should be so, she reached forth and touched his black head, and it became snowy white, and all the birds cried 'Long live the king!'

"Then Old Mother Nature turned to tiny Mr. Hummer and touched his throat, and behold a shining ruby was there, the reward of loyalty, faith, and bravery.

"Then King Eagle mounted into the air and proudly led the way to the promised land. And so the birds went forth and peopled the Great World, and King Eagle and his children and his children's children have ruled the air ever since and have worn the snowy crown which King Eagle of long ago so bravely won."

II

HOW OLD MR. MINK TAUGHT HIMSELF TO SWIM

II

HOW OLD MR. MINK TAUGHT HIMSELF TO SWIM

OF all the little people who live in the Green Forest or on the Green Meadows or around the Smiling Pool, Billy Mink has the most accomplishments. At least, it seems that way to his friends and neighbors. He can run very swiftly; he can climb very nimbly; his eyes and his ears and his nose are all wonderfully keen, and—he can swim like a fish. Yes, Sir, Billy Mink is just as much at home in the water as out of it. So, wherever he happens to be, in the Green Forest, out on the Green Meadows, along the Laughing Brook, or in the Smiling

Pool, he feels perfectly at home and quite able to look out for himself.

Once Billy Mink had boasted that he could do anything that any one else who wore fur could do, but boasters almost always come to grief, and Grandfather Frog had brought Billy to grief that time. He had invited every one to meet at the Smiling Pool and see Billy Mink do whatever any one else who wore fur could do, and then, when Billy had run and jumped and climbed and swum, Grandfather Frog had called Flitter the Bat. There was some one wearing fur who could fly, and of course Billy Mink couldn't do that. It cured Billy of boasting,—for a while, anyway.

Now Peter Rabbit, who can do little but run and jump, used sometimes to feel a wee bit of envy in his heart when he thought of all the things that Billy

Mink could do and do well. Somehow Peter could never make it seem quite right that one person should be able to do so many things when others could do only one or two things. He said as much to Grandfather Frog one day, as they watched Billy Mink catch a fat trout.

"Chug-a-rum!" said Grandfather Frog and looked sharply at Peter. "Chug-a-rum! People never know what they can do till they try. Once upon a time Billy Mink's great-great-ever-so-great-grandfather couldn't swim any more than you can, but he didn't waste any time foolishly wishing that he could."

"What did he do?" asked Peter eagerly.

"Learned how," replied Grandfather Frog gruffly. "Made it his business to learn how. Then he taught his children, and they taught their children, and after a long time it came natural to the Mink family to swim."

"Did it take old Mr. Mink very long to learn how?" asked Peter wistfully.

"Quite a while," replied Grandfather Frog. "Quite a while. Perhaps you would like to hear about it."

"Oh, if you please, Grandfather Frog," cried Peter. "If you please. I should love dearly to hear about it. Perhaps then I can learn to swim."

Grandfather Frog snapped up a foolish green fly that happened his way, and Peter heard something that sounded very much like a chuckle. He looked at Grandfather Frog suspiciously. Was that chuckle because of the foolish green fly, or was Grandfather Frog laughing at him? Peter wasn't sure.

"It all happened a long time ago

when the world was young, as a great many other things happened," began Grandfather Frog. "Old Mr. Mink, the ever-so-great-grandfather of Billy Mink, couldn't do all the things that Billy can now. For instance, he couldn't swim. But he could do a great many things, and he was very smart. It has always run in the Mink family to be smart. He dressed very much as Billy does now, except that he didn't have the waterproof coat that Billy has. And he was a great traveler, just as Billy is. Everybody smaller than he and some who were bigger were a little bit afraid of old Mr. Mink, for he was quite as sly and cunning as Mr. Fox, and it was suspected that he knew a great deal more than he ever admitted about eggs that were stolen and nests that were broken up, and other strange things that happened in the Green Forest and along the Laughing Brook. But he never was caught doing anything wrong and always seemed to be minding his own business, so, all things considered, he got along very well with his neighbors.

"Now Mr. Mink was small and spry, and his wits were as nimble as his feet. He saw all that was going on about him, and he was wise enough to keep his tongue still, so that it never got him into trouble as gossipy tongues do some people I know."

Peter Rabbit fidgeted uneasily. It seemed to him that Grandfather Frog had looked at him very hard when he said this. But Grandfather Frog just cleared his throat and went on with his story.

"Yes, Sir, old Mr. Mink kept his eyes wide open and his ears wide open and the wits in his little brown head always working. He noticed that those who were fussy about what they ate and insisted on having a special kind of food often went hungry or had to hunt long and hard to find what they liked, so he made up his mind to learn to eat many kinds of food. This is how it happens that he learned to like fish. His big cousin, Mr. Otter, often caught a bigger fish than he could eat all himself and would leave some of it on the bank. Mr. Mink would find it and help himself.

"But having to depend on Mr. Otter to get the fish for him didn't suit Mr. Mink at all. In the first place, he didn't have as much as he wanted. And then again he didn't have it when he wanted it. 'If I could learn to catch fish for myself, I would be much better off,' thought Mr. Mink. After this he spent a great deal of time on the banks of the

Smiling Pool watching Mr. Otter swim to see just how he did it. 'If he can swim, I can swim,' said Mr. Mink to himself, and went off up the Laughing Brook to a quiet little pool where the water was not deep.

"At first he didn't like it at all. The water got in his ears and up his nose and choked him. And then it was so dreadfully wet! But he would grit his teeth and keep at it. After a while he got so that he could paddle around a little. Gradually he lost his fear of the water. Then he found that because he naturally moved so quickly he could sometimes catch foolish minnows who swam in where the water was very shallow. This was great sport, and he quite often had fish for dinner now.

"But he wasn't satisfied. No, Sir, he wasn't satisfied. Whatever Mr. Mink did, he wanted to do well. He could run well and climb well, and there was no better hunter in all the Green Forest. He was bound that he would swim well. So he kept trying and trying. He learned to fill his lungs with air and hold his breath for a long time, while he swam as fast as ever he could with his head under water as he had seen his cousin, Mr. Otter, swim. The more he did this, the longer he could hold his breath. After a while he found that because he was slim and trim and moved so fast, he could outswim Mr. Muskrat, and this made him feel very good indeed, for Mr. Muskrat spent nearly all his time in the water and was accounted a very good swimmer. There was only one thing that bothered Mr. Mink. The water was so dreadfully wet! Every time he came out of it, he had to run his hardest to dry off and keep from getting cold. This was very tiresome and he did wish that there was an easier way of drying off.

"Then came the bad time, the sad time, when food was scarce, and most of the little people in the Green Forest and on the Green Meadow went hungry. But Mr. Mink didn't go hungry. Oh, my, no! You see, he had learned to catch fish, and so he had plenty to eat. When Old Mother Nature came to see how all the little people were getting along, she was very much surprised to find that Mr. Mink had become a famous swimmer. She watched him catch a fish. Then she watched him run about to dry off and keep from getting cold, and her eyes twinkled.

"'He who helps himself deserves to be helped,' said Old Mother Nature. Mr. Mink didn't know what she meant by that, but the next morning he found out. Yes, Sir, the next morning he found out. He found that he had a brand new coat over his old one, and the new one was waterproof. He could swim as much as he pleased and not get the least bit wet, because the water couldn't get through that new coat. And ever since that long-ago day when the world was young, the Minks have had waterproof coats and have been famous fishermen. Hello, Peter Rabbit! What under the sun are you trying to do, swelling yourself up that way?"

"I—I was just practising holding my breath," replied Peter and looked very, very foolish.

"Ho, ho, ho! Ha, ha, ha!" laughed Grandfather Frog. "You can't learn to swim by holding your breath on dry land, Peter Rabbit."

III

HOW OLD MR. TOAD LEARNED TO SING

III

HOW OLD MR. TOAD LEARNED TO SING

PETER RABBIT never will forget how he laughed the first time he heard Old Mr. Toad say that he could sing and was going to sing. Why, Peter would as soon think of singing himself, and that is something he can no more do than he can fly. Peter had known Old Mr. Toad ever since he could remember. He was rather fond of him, even if he did play jokes on him once in a while. But he always thought of Old Mr. Toad as one of the homeliest of all his friends,—slow, awkward, and too commonplace to be very interesting. So when, in the glad joyousness of the spring, Old Mr. Toad had told Jimmy Skunk that he was going down to the Smiling Pool to sing because without him the great chorus there would lack one of its sweetest voices, Peter and Jimmy had laughed till the tears came.

A few days later Peter happened over to the Smiling Pool for a call on Grandfather Frog. A mighty chorus of joy from unseen singers rose from all about the Smiling Pool. Peter knew about those singers. They were Hylas, the little cousins of Sticky-toes the Tree Toad. Peter sat very still on the edge of the bank trying to see one of them. Suddenly he became aware of a new note, one he never had noticed before and sweeter than any of the others. Indeed it was one of the sweetest of all the spring songs, as sweet as the love notes of Tommy Tit the Chickadee, than which there is none sweeter.

It seemed to come from the shallow water just in front of Peter, and he looked eagerly for the singer. Then his eyes opened until it seemed as if they would pop right out of his head, and he dropped his lower jaw foolishly. There was Old Mr. Toad with a queer bag Peter never had seen before swelled out under his chin, and as surely as Peter was sitting on that bank, it was Old Mr. Toad who was the sweet singer!

Old Mr. Toad paid no attention to Peter, not even when he was spoken to. He was so absorbed in his singing that he just didn't hear. Peter sat there a while to listen; then he called Jimmy Skunk and Unc' Billy Possum, who were also listening to the music, and they were just as surprised as Peter. Then he spied Jerry Muskrat at the other end of the Smiling Pool and hurried over there. Peter was so full of the discovery he had made that he could think of nothing else. He fairly ached to tell.

"Jerry!" he cried. "Oh, Jerry Muskrat! Do you know that Old Mr. Toad can sing?"

Jerry looked surprised that Peter should ask such a question. "Of course I know it," said he. "It would be mighty funny if I didn't know it, seeing that he is the sweetest singer in the Smiling Pool and has sung here every spring since I can remember."

Peter looked very much chagrined. "I didn't know it until just now," he confessed. "I didn't believe him when he told me that he could sing. I wonder how he ever learned."

"He didn't learn any more than you learned how to jump," replied Jerry. "It just came to him naturally. His father sang, and his grandfather, and his great grandfather, way back to the beginning of things. I thought everybody knew about that."

"I don't. Tell me about it. Please do, Jerry," begged Peter.

"All right, I will," replied Jerry good-naturedly. "It's something you ought to know about, anyway. In the first place, Old Mr. Toad belongs to a very old and honorable family, one of the very oldest. I've heard say that it goes way back almost to the very beginning of things when there wasn't much land. Anyway, the first Toad, the great-great-ever-so-great-grand-father of Old Mr. Toad and own cousin to the great-great-ever-so-great-grand-father of Grandfather Frog, was one of the first to leave the water for the dry land.

"Old Mother Nature met him hopping along and making hard work of it because, of course, it was so new. She looked at him sharply. 'What are you doing here?' she demanded. 'Aren't you contented with the water where you were born?'

"Mr. Toad bowed very low. 'Yes'm,' said he very humbly. 'I'll go right back there if you say so. I thought there must be some things worth finding out on the land, and that I might be of some use in the Great World.'

"His answer pleased Old Mother Nature. She was worried. She had planted all kinds of things on the land, and they were springing up everywhere, but she had discovered that bugs of many kinds liked the tender green things and were increasing so fast and were so greedy that they threatened to strip the land of all that she had planted. She had so many things to attend to that she hadn't time to take care of the bugs. 'If you truly want to be of some use,' said she, 'you can attend to some of those bugs.'

"Mr. Toad went right to work, and Old Mother Nature went about some other business. Having so many other things to look after, she quite forgot about Mr. Toad, and it was several weeks before she came that way again. Right in the middle of a great bare place where the bugs had eaten everything was a beautiful green spot, and patiently hopping from plant to plant was Mr. Toad, snapping up every bug he could see. He didn't see Old Mother Nature and kept right on working. She watched him a while as he hopped from plant to plant catching bugs as fast as he could, and then she spoke.

"'Have you stayed right here ever since I last saw you?' she asked.

"Mr. Toad gave a start of surprise. 'Yes'm,' said he.

"'But I thought you wanted to see the Great World and learn things,' said she.

"Mr. Toad looked a little embarrassed. 'So I did,' he replied, 'but I wanted to be of some use, and the bugs have kept me so busy there was no time to travel. Besides, I have learned a great deal right here. I—I couldn't get around fast enough to save *all* the plants, but I have saved what I could.'

"Old Mother Nature was more pleased than she was willing to show, for Mr. Toad was the first of all the little people who had tried to help her, and he had done what he could willingly and faithfully.

"'I suppose,' said she, speaking a little gruffly, 'you expect me to reward you.'

"Mr. Toad looked surprised and a little hurt. 'I don't want any reward,' said he. 'I didn't do it for that. It will be reward enough to know that I really have helped and to be allowed to continue to help.'

"At that Old Mother Nature's face lighted with one of her most beautiful smiles. 'Mr. Toad,' said she, 'if you could have just what you want, what would it be?'

"Mr. Toad hesitated a few minutes and then said shyly, 'A beautiful voice.'

"It was Old Mother Nature's turn to look surprised. 'A beautiful voice!' she exclaimed. 'Pray, why do you want a beautiful voice?'

"'So that I can express my happiness in the most beautiful way I know of,—by singing,' replied Mr. Toad.

"'You shall have it,' declared Old Mother Nature, 'but not all the time lest you be tempted to forget your work, which, you know, is the real source of true happiness. In the spring of each year you shall go back to your home in the water, and there for a time you shall sing to your heart's content, and there shall be no sweeter voice than yours.'

" Sure enough, when the next spring came, Mr. Toad was filled with a great longing to go home. When he got there, he found that in his throat was a little music bag; and when he swelled it out, he had one of the sweetest voices in the world. And so it has been ever since with the Toad family. Old Mr. Toad is one of the sweetest singers in the Smiling Pool, but when it is time to go back to work he never grumbles, but is one of the most faithful workers in Mother Nature's garden," concluded Jerry Muskrat.

Peter sighed. "I never could work," said he. "Perhaps that is why I cannot sing."

"Very likely," replied Jerry Muskrat, quite forgetting that he cannot sing himself although he is a great worker.

IV

HOW OLD MR. CROW LOST HIS DOUBLE TONGUE

IV

HOW OLD MR. CROW LOST HIS DOUBLE TONGUE

"CAW, caw, caw, caw!" Blacky the Crow sat in the top of a tall tree and seemed trying to see just how much noise he could make with that harsh voice of his. Peter Rabbit peered out from the dear Old Briar-patch and frowned.

"If I had a voice as unpleasant as that, I'd forget I could talk. Yes, Sir, I'd forget I had a tongue," declared Peter.

Somebody laughed, and Peter turned quickly to find Jimmy Skunk. "What are you laughing at?" demanded Peter.

"At the idea of you forgetting that you had a tongue," replied Jimmy.

"Well, I would if I had a voice like Blacky's," persisted Peter, although he grinned a wee bit foolishly as he looked at Jimmy Skunk, for you know Peter is a great gossip.

"It's lucky for you that you haven't then," retorted Jimmy. "I'm afraid that you would lose your tongue just as old Mr. Crow did."

That sounded like a story. Right away Peter sat up and took notice. "Did old Mr. Crow really lose his tongue? How did he lose it? Why did he lose it? When—"

Jimmy Skunk clapped a hand over each ear and pretended that he was going to run away. Peter jumped in front of him. "No, you don't!" he cried. "You've just got to tell me that story, Jimmy Skunk."

"What story?" asked Jimmy, as if he hadn't the least idea in the world what Peter was talking about, though of course he knew perfectly well.

"Caw, caw, caw, caw!" shouted Blacky the Crow from the distant treetop.

"The story of how old Mr. Crow lost his tongue. You may as well tell me first as last, because I'll give you no peace until you do," insisted Peter.

Jimmy grinned. "If that's the case, I guess I'll have to," said he. "Wait until I find a comfortable place to sit down. I never could tell a story standing up."

At last he found a place to suit him and after changing his position two or three times to make sure that he was perfectly comfortable, he began.

"Once upon a time—"

"Never mind about that," interrupted Peter. "I don't see why all stories have to begin 'Once upon a time.' It seems as if everything interesting happened long ago."

"If you don't watch out, this story won't begin at all," declared Jimmy.

Peter looked properly ashamed for interrupting, and Jimmy started again.

"Once upon a time old Mr. Crow, the great-great-ever-so-great-grandfather of Blacky, over there, possessed the most wonderful tongue of any of the little people who ran, walked, crawled, or flew. He could imitate any and everybody, and he did. He could sing like Mr. Meadow Lark, or he could bark like Mr. Wolf. He could whistle like Mr. Quail, or he could growl like old King Bear. There wasn't anybody whose voice he couldn't imitate and do it so well that if you had been there and heard but not seen him, you never would have guessed that it was an imitation.

"Now the imp of mischief was in old Mr. Crow, just as it is in Blacky to-day, and he was smart too. There wasn't anybody smarter than old Mr. Crow. It's from him that Blacky gets his smartness. It didn't take him long to discover that no one else had such a wonderful tongue. It was even more wonderful than the tongue of old Mr. Mocker the Mocking Bird. Mr. Mocker could imitate the songs of other birds, but old Mr. Crow could imitate anybody, as I have said. He puzzled over it a good deal himself for a while. He couldn't understand how he could make any sound he pleased, while his neighbors could make only a few special sounds.

"Being very smart and shrewd, just as Blacky is, he finally made up his mind that it must be in his tongue. As soon as he thought of that, he started out to find out, and on one excuse or another he managed to get all his neighbors to show him their tongues. Sure enough, his own tongue was different from any of the others. It was split a little, so that it was almost like two tongues in one.

"'That's it,' he chuckled. 'I knew it. It's this little old tongue of mine. Nobody else has got one like it, but nobody knows that but me. I must make good use of it. Yes, Sir, I must make good use of it.'

"Now when old Mr. Crow said that, he didn't really mean good use at all. That is, he didn't mean what you or I or any of his neighbors would have called good use. What he did mean was the use that would bring to himself the greatest gain in pleasure, and being a great joker, he began by having a lot of fun with his neighbors. When he saw Mr. Rabbit, your grandfather a thousand times removed, coming along, he would hide, and just as Mr. Rabbit was passing, he would snarl like Mr. Lynx. Of course Mr. Rabbit would be scared almost to death, and away he would go, lipperty-lipperty-lip, and old Mr. Crow would laugh so that he had to hold his black sides. He would hide in the top of a tree near Mr. Squirrel's home, and just when Mr. Squirrel had found a fat nut and started to eat it, he would scream like Mr. Hawk and then laugh to see Mr. Squirrel drop his nut and dive headfirst into the nearest hole. He would squeak like a mouse when Mr. Fox was passing, just to see Mr. Fox hunt and hunt for the dinner he felt sure was close at hand.

"But after a while Mr. Crow wasn't satisfied with harmless jokes. Times were getting hard, and everybody had to work to get enough to eat. This didn't suit Mr. Crow at all, and one day when he chanced to discover one of his neighbors just sitting down to a good meal, a new idea came to him. He stole as near as he could without being seen and suddenly growled like old King Bear. Of course that meal was left in a hurry. 'It is too bad to see all that good food go to waste,' said Mr. Crow and promptly ate it.

"After that, instead of hunting for food himself, he just kept a sharp eye on his neighbors, and when they had found something he wanted, he frightened them away and helped himself. All the time he was so sly about it that never once was he suspected. He was a great talker, was Mr. Crow, and spent a great deal of time gossiping, and he was always one of the first to offer sympathy to those who had lost a meal.

"Now all this time, unknown to old Mr. Crow, Old Mother Nature knew just what was going on, for you can't fool her, and it's of no use to try. One morning Mr. Crow discovered Mr. Coon just sitting down to a good breakfast. He stole up behind Mr. Coon and opened his mouth to bark like Mr. Coyote, but instead of a bark, there came forth a harsh 'Caw, caw, caw.' It is a question which was the more surprised, Mr. Coon or Mr. Crow. Mr. Coon didn't forget his manners. He politely invited Mr. Crow to sit down and take breakfast with him. But Mr. Crow had lost his appetite. Somehow his tongue felt very queer. He thanked Mr. Coon and begged to be excused. Then he hurried over to the nearest pool of water in which he could see his reflection and stuck out his tongue. It was no longer split into a double tongue. Then old Mr. Crow guessed that Old Mother Nature had found him out and punished him, but to make sure, he flew to the most lonesome place he knew of, and there he tried to imitate the voices of his neighbors; but try as he would, all he could say was 'Caw, caw, caw.'

"For a long, long time after that no one ever heard Mr. Crow say a word. His neighbors didn't know what to make of it, for you remember he had been a great gossip. They said that he must have lost his tongue. Of course he hadn't, but he felt that he might as well have. And ever since then the Crow family has had the harshest of all voices."

"Caw, caw, caw!" shouted Blacky from the top of the tree where he was sitting.

"I wonder," said Peter Rabbit

thoughtfully, " if he could imitate other people if his tongue should be split."

" I've heard say that he could," replied Jimmy Skunk, " but I don't know. One thing is sure, and that is that he is just as smart and sly as his great - great - ever - so - great - grandfather was, and I guess it is just as well that his tongue is just as it is."

V

HOW HOWLER THE WOLF GOT HIS NAME

V

HOW HOWLER THE WOLF GOT HIS NAME

PETER RABBIT never had seen Howler the Wolf, but he had heard his voice in the distance, and the mere sound had given him cold shivers. It just went all through him. It was very different from the voice of Old Man Coyote. The latter is bad enough, sounding as it does like many voices, but there is not in it that terrible fierceness which the voice of his big cousin contains. Peter had no desire to hear it any nearer. The first time he met his cousin, Jumper the Hare, he asked him about Howler, for Jumper had come down to the Green Forest from the Great Woods where Howler lives and is feared.

"Did you hear him?" exclaimed Jumper. "I hope he won't take it into his head to come down here. I don't believe he will, because it is too near the homes of men. If the sound of his voice way off there gave you cold shivers, I'm afraid you'd shake all to pieces if you heard him close by. He's just as fierce as his voice sounds. There is one thing about him that I like, though, and that is that he gives fair warning when he is hunting. He doesn't come sneaking about without a sound, like Tufty the Lynx. He hunts like Bowser the Hound and lets you know that he is out hunting. Did you ever hear how he got his name?"

"No. How did he get his name?" asked Peter eagerly.

"Well, of course it's a family name now and is handed down and has been for years and years, ever since the first

Wolf began hunting way back when the world was young," explained Jumper. "For a long time the first Wolf had no name. Most of the other animals and birds had names, but nothing seemed to just fit the big gray Wolf. He looked a great deal like his cousin, Mr. Dog, and still more like his other cousin, Mr. Coyote. But he was stronger than either, could run farther and faster than either, and had quite as wonderful a nose as either.

"With Mr. Wolf, as with all the other animals, life was an easy matter at first. There was plenty to eat, and everybody was on good terms with everybody else. But there came a time, as you know, when food became scarce. It was then that the big learned to hunt the small, and fear was born into the world. Mr. Wolf was swift of leg and keen of nose. His teeth were long and sharp, and he was so strong that there were few he feared to fight with. In fact, he didn't know fear at all, for he simply kept out of the way of those who were too big and strong for him to fight.

"Most people like to do the things they know they can do well. Mr. Wolf early learned the joy of hunting. I can't understand it myself. Can you?"

Peter shook his head. You see neither Jumper nor Peter ever have hunted any one in all their lives. It is always they who are hunted.

"Perhaps it was because he was so strong of wind and leg that he enjoyed running, and because he was so keen of nose that he enjoyed following a trail. Anyway, he scorned to spend his time sneaking about as did his cousin, Mr. Coyote, but chose to follow the swiftest runners and to match his nose and speed and skill against their speed and wits. He didn't bother to hunt little people like us when there were big people like Mr. Deer. The longer and harder the hunt, the more Mr. Wolf seemed to enjoy it.

"At first he hunted silently, running swiftly with his nose to the ground. But this gave the ones he hunted very little chance; he was upon them before they even suspected that he was on their trail. It always made Mr. Wolf feel mean. He never could hold his head and his tail up after that kind of a hunt. He felt so like a sneak that he just had to put his tail between his legs for very shame. There was nothing to be proud about in such a hunt.

"One night he sat thinking about it. Gentle Mistress Moon looked down at him through the tree-tops, and something inside him urged him to tell her his troubles. He pointed his sharp nose up at her, opened his mouth and, because she was so far away, did his best to make her hear. That was the very first Wolf howl ever heard. There was something very lonely and shivery and terrible in the sound, and all who heard it shook with fear. Mr. Wolf didn't know this, but he did know that he felt better for howling. So every night he pointed his nose up at Mistress Moon and howled.

"It happened that once as he did this, a Deer jumped at the first sound and rushed away in great fright. This gave Mr. Wolf an idea. The next day when he went hunting he threw up his head and howled at the very first smell of fresh tracks. That day he had the longest hunt he ever had known, for the Deer had had fair warning. Mr. Wolf didn't get the Deer, because the latter swam across a lake and so got away, but he returned home in high spirits in spite of an empty stomach. You see, he felt that it had been a fair hunt. After that he always gave fair warning. As he ran, he howled for very joy. No longer did he carry his bushy tail between his legs, for no longer did he feel like a coward and a sneak. Instead, he carried it proudly. Of all the animals who hunted, he was the only one who gave fair warning, and he felt that he had a right to be proud. All the others hunted by stealth. He alone hunted openly and boldly.

"Now this earned for him first the dislike and then the hatred of the other hunters. You see, when he was hunting, he spoiled the hunting of those who stole soft-footed through the Green Forest and caught their victims by surprise. The little people heard his voice and either hid away or were on guard, so that it was hard work for the silent hunters to surprise them. At the sound of his hunting cry, old King Bear, who was king no longer, would growl a deep, rumbly-grumbly growl, though he didn't mind so much as some, because he did very little hunting. He wouldn't have done any if food had not been so scarce, because he would have been entirely satisfied with berries and roots, if he could have found enough. Mr. Lynx and Mr. Panther would snarl angrily. Mr. Coyote and Mr. Fox would show their teeth and mutter about what they would do to Mr. Wolf if only they were big enough and strong enough and brave enough.

"Of course, it wasn't long before Mr. Wolf discovered that he had no friends. The little people feared him, and the big people hated him because he spoiled

"Old King Bear, who was king no longer, would grow a deep, rumbly-grumbly growl."

their hunting. But he didn't mind. In fact, he looked down on Mr. Lynx and Mr. Panther and Mr. Coyote and Mr. Fox, and when he met them, he lifted his tail a little more proudly than ever. Sometimes he would howl out of pure mischief just to spoil the hunting of the others. So, little by little, he began to be spoken of as Howler the Wolf, and after a while everybody called him Howler.

"Of course, Howler taught his children how to hunt and that the only honorable and fair way was to give those they hunted fair warning. So it grew to be a fixed habit of the Wolf family to give fair warning that they were abroad and then trust to their wind and wits and speed and noses to catch those they were after. The result was that they grew strong, able to travel long distances, keen of nose, and sharp of wit. Because the big people hated them, and the little people feared them, they lived by themselves and so formed the habit of hunting together for company.

"It has been so ever since, and the name Howler has been handed down to this day. No sound in all the Great Woods carries with it more fear than does the voice of Howler the Wolf, and no one hunts so openly, boldly, and honorably. Be thankful, Peter, that Howler never comes down to the Green Forest, but stays far from the homes of men."

"I am," replied Peter. "Just the same, I think he deserves a better name for the fair way in which he hunts, though his name certainly does fit him. I would a lot rather be caught by some one who had given me fair warning than by some one who came sneaking after me and gave me no warning. But I don't want to be caught at all, so I think I'll hurry back to the dear Old Briar-patch." And Peter did.

VI

HOW OLD MR. SQUIRREL BECAME THRIFTY

VI

HOW OLD MR. SQUIRREL BECAME THRIFTY

GRANDFATHER FROG sat on his big green lily-pad in the Smiling Pool and shook his head reprovingly at Peter Rabbit. Peter is such a happy-go-lucky little fellow that he never thinks of anything but the good time he can have in the present. He never looks ahead to the future. So of course Peter seldom worries. If the sun shines to-day, Peter takes it for granted that it will shine to-morrow; so he hops and skips and has a good time and just trusts to luck.

Now Grandfather Frog is very old and very wise, and he doesn't believe in luck. No, Sir, Grandfather Frog doesn't believe in luck.

"Chug-a-rum!" says Grandfather Frog, "Luck never just *happens.* What people call bad luck is just the result of their own foolishness or carelessness or both, and what people call good luck is just the result of their own wisdom and carefulness and common sense."

Peter Rabbit had been making fun of Happy Jack Squirrel because Happy Jack said that he had too much to do to stop and play that morning. Here it was summer, and winter was a long way off. What was summer for if not to play in and have a good time? Yet Happy Jack was already thinking of winter and was hunting for a new storehouse so as to have it ready when the time to fill it with nuts should come. It was much better to play and take sun-naps among the buttercups and daisies and just have a good time all day long.

"Chug-a-rum!" said Grandfather Frog, "Did you ever hear how old Mr. Squirrel learned thrift?"

"No," cried Peter Rabbit, stretching himself out in the soft grass on the edge of the Smiling Pool. "Do tell us about it. Please do, Grandfather Frog!"

You know Peter dearly loves a story. All the other little meadow and forest people who were about the Smiling Pool joined Peter Rabbit in begging Grandfather Frog for the story, and after they had teased for it a long time (Grandfather Frog dearly loves to be teased), he cleared his throat and began.

"Once upon a time when the world was young, in the days when old King Bear ruled in the Green Forest, everybody had to take King Bear presents of things to eat. That was because he was king. You know kings never have to work like other people to get enough to eat; everybody brings them a little of their best, and so kings have the best in the land without the trouble of working for it. It was just this way with old King Bear. That was before he grew so fat and lazy and selfish that Old Mother Nature declared that he should be king no longer.

"Now in those days lived old Mr. Squirrel, the grandfather a thousand times removed of Happy Jack Squirrel whom you all know. Of course, he wasn't old then. He was young and frisky, just like Happy Jack, and he was a great favorite with old King Bear. He was a saucy fellow, was Mr. Squirrel, and he used to spend most of his time playing tricks on the other meadow and forest people. He even dared to play jokes on old King Bear. Sometimes old King Bear would lose his temper, and then Mr. Squirrel would whisk up in the top of a tall tree and keep out of sight until old King Bear had recovered his good nature.

"Those were happy days, very happy days indeed, and old King Bear was a very wise ruler. There was plenty of everything to eat, and so nobody missed the little they brought to old King Bear. Having so much brought to him, he grew very particular. Yes, Sir, old King Bear grew very particular indeed. Some began to whisper behind his back that he was fussy. He would pick out the very best of everything for himself and give the rest to his family and special friends or else just let it go to waste.

"Now old King Bear was very fond

of lively little Mr. Squirrel, and often he would give Mr. Squirrel some of the good things for which he had no room in his own stomach. Mr. Squirrel was smart. He soon found out that the more he amused old King Bear, the more of King Bear's good things he had. It was a lot easier to get his living this way than to hunt for his food as he always had in the past. Besides, it was a lot more fun. So little Mr. Squirrel studied how to please old King Bear, and he grew fat on the good things which other people had earned.

"One day old King Bear gave little Mr. Squirrel six big, fat nuts. You see, old King Bear didn't care for nuts himself, not the kind with the hard shells, anyway, so he really wasn't as generous as he seemed, which is the way with a great many people. It is easy to give what you don't want yourself.

Little Mr. Squirrel bowed very low and thanked old King Bear in his best manner. He really didn't want those nuts, for his stomach was full at the time, but it wouldn't do to refuse a gift from the king. So he took the nuts and pretended to be delighted with them.

" 'What shall I do with them?' said little Mr. Squirrel as soon as he was alone. 'It won't do for me to leave them where old King Bear will find them, for it might make him very angry.' At last he remembered a certain hollow tree. 'The very place!' cried little Mr. Squirrel. 'I'll drop them in there, and no one will be any the wiser.'

"No sooner thought of than it was done, and little Mr. Squirrel frisked away in his usual happy-go-lucky fashion and forgot all about the nuts in the hollow tree. It wasn't very long after this that Old Mother Nature began to hear complaints of old King Bear and his rule in the Green Forest. He had grown fat and lazy, and all his relatives had grown fat and lazy because, you see, none of them had to work for the things they ate. The little forest and meadow people were growing tired of feeding the Bear family. It was just at the beginning of winter when Old Mother Nature came to see for herself what the trouble was. It didn't take her long to find out. No, Sir, it didn't take her long. You can't fool Old Mother Nature, and it's of no use to try. She took one good look at old King Bear nodding in the cave where he used to sleep. He was so fat he looked as if he would burst his skin.

"Old Mother Nature frowned. 'You are such a lazy fellow that you shall be king no longer. Instead, you shall sleep all winter and grow thin and thinner till you awake in the spring, and then you will have to hunt for your own food, for never again shall you live on the gifts of others,' said she.

"All the little forest and meadow people who had been bringing tribute, that is things to eat, to old King Bear rejoiced that they need do so no longer and went about their business. All of old King Bear's family, including his cousin Mr. Coon, had been put to sleep just like old King Bear himself. Yes, Sir, they were all asleep, fast asleep.

"Little Mr. Squirrel felt lonesome. He grew more lonesome every day. None of the other little people would have anything to do with him because they remembered how he had lived without working when he was the favorite of King Bear. The weather was cold, and it was hard work to find anything to eat. Mr. Squirrel was hungry all the time. He couldn't think of anything but his stomach and how empty it was. He grew thin and thinner.

"One cold day when the snow covered the earth, little Mr. Squirrel went without breakfast. Then he went without dinner. You see, he couldn't find so much as a pine-seed to eat. Late in the afternoon he crept into a hollow tree to get away from the cold, bitter wind. He was very tired and very cold and very, very hungry. Tears filled his eyes and ran over and dripped from his nose. He curled up on the leaves at the bottom of the hollow to try to go to sleep and forget. Under him was something hard. He twisted and turned, but he couldn't get in a comfortable position. Finally he looked to see what the trouble was caused by. What do you think he found? Six big, fat nuts! Yes, Sir, six big, fat nuts! Little Mr.

Squirrel was so glad that he cried for very joy.

"When he had eaten two, he felt better and decided to keep the others for the next day. Then he began to wonder how those nuts happened to be in that hollow tree. He thought and thought, and at last he remembered how he had hidden six nuts in this very hollow a long time before, when he had had more than he knew what to do with. These were the very nuts, the present of old King Bear.

"Right then as he thought about it, little Mr. Squirrel had a bright idea. He made up his mind that thereafter he would stop his happy-go-lucky idleness, and the first time that ever he found plenty of food, he would fill that hollow tree just as full as he could pack it, and then if there should come a time when food was scarce, he would have plenty. And that is just what he did do. The next fall when nuts were plentiful, he worked from morning till night storing them away in the hollow tree, and all that winter he was happy and fat, for he had plenty to eat. He never had to beg of any one. He had learned to save.

"And ever since then the Squirrels have been among the wisest of all the little forest people and always the busiest.

"The Squirrel family long since learned
That things are best when duly earned;
That play and fun are found in work
By him who does not try to shirk.

"And that's all," finished Grandfather Frog.

"Thank you! Thank you, Grandfather Frog!" cried Peter Rabbit.

VII

HOW LIGHTFOOT THE DEER LEARNED TO JUMP

VII

HOW LIGHTFOOT THE DEER LEARNED TO JUMP

IT isn't often that Peter Rabbit is filled with envy. As a rule, Peter is very free from anything like envy. Usually he is quite content with the gifts bestowed upon him by Old Mother Nature, and if others have more than he has, he is glad for them and wastes no time fretting because he has not been so fortunate. But once in a great while Peter becomes really and truly envious. It was that way the first time he saw Lightfoot the Deer leap over a fallen tree, and ever after, when he saw Lightfoot, a little of that same feeling stirred in his heart. You see, Peter always had been very proud of his own powers of jumping. To be sure Jumper the Hare could jump higher and farther than he could, but Jumper is his own cousin, so it was all in the family, so to speak, and Peter didn't mind. But to see Lightfoot the Deer go sailing over the tops of the bushes and over the fallen trees as if he had springs in his legs was quite another matter.

"I wish I could jump like that," said Peter right out loud one day, as he stood with his hands on his hips watching Lightfoot leap over a pile of brush.

"Why don't you learn to?" asked Jimmy Skunk with a mischievous twinkle in the eye which Peter couldn't see. "Lightfoot couldn't always jump like that; he had to learn. Why don't you find out how? Probably Grandfather Frog knows all about it. He knows about almost everything. If I were you, I'd ask him."

"I—I—I don't just like to," replied Peter. "I've asked him so many questions that I am afraid he'll think me a nuisance. I tell you what, Jimmy, you ask him!" Peter's eyes brightened as he said this.

Jimmy chuckled. "No, you don't!" said he. "If there is anything you want to know from Grandfather Frog, ask him yourself. I don't want to know how Lightfoot learned to jump. He may jump over the moon, for all I care. Have you seen any fat beetles this morning, Peter?"

"No," replied Peter shortly. "I'm not interested in beetles. There may never be any fat beetles, for all I care."

Jimmy laughed. It was a good-natured, chuckling kind of a laugh. "Don't get huffy, Peter," said he.

"Here's hoping that you learn how to jump like Lightfoot the Deer, and that I get a stomachful of fat beetles." With that Jimmy Skunk slowly ambled along down the Crooked Little Path.

Peter watched him out of sight, sighed, started for the dear Old Briar-patch, stopped, sighed again, and then headed straight for the Smiling Pool. Grandfather Frog was there on his big green lily-pad, and Peter wasted no time.

"How did Lightfoot the Deer learn to jump so splendidly, Grandfather Frog?" he blurted out almost before he had stopped running.

Grandfather Frog blinked his great, goggly eyes. "Chug-a-rum!" said he. "If you'll jump across the Laughing Brook over there where it comes into the Smiling Pool, I'll tell you."

Peter looked at the Laughing Brook

in dismay. It was quite wide at that point. "I—I can't," he stammered.

"Then I can't tell you how Lightfoot learned to jump," replied Grandfather Frog, quite as if the matter were settled.

"I—I'll try!" Peter hastened to blurt out.

"All right. While you are trying, I'll see if I can remember the story," replied Grandfather Frog.

Peter went back a little so as to get a good start. Then he ran as hard as he knew how, and when he reached the bank of the Laughing Brook, he jumped with all his might. It was a good jump—a splendid jump—but it wasn't quite enough of a jump, and Peter landed with a great splash in the water! Grandfather Frog opened his great mouth as wide as he could, which is very wide indeed, and laughed until the tears rolled down from his great, goggly eyes. Jerry Muskrat and Billy Mink rolled over and over on the bank, laughing until their sides ached. Even Spotty the Turtle smiled, which is very unusual for Spotty.

Now Peter does not like the water, and though he can swim, he doesn't feel at all at home in it. He paddled for the shore as fast as he could, and in his heart was something very like anger. No one likes to be laughed at. Peter intended to start for home the very minute he reached the shore. But just before his feet touched bottom, he heard the great, deep voice of Grandfather Frog.

"That is just the way Lightfoot the Deer learned to jump—trying to do what he couldn't do and keeping at it until he could. It all happened a great while ago when the world was young."

Grandfather Frog was talking quite as if nothing had happened, and he had never thought of laughing. Peter was so put out that he wanted to keep right on, but he just couldn't miss that story. His curiosity wouldn't let him. So he shook himself and then lay down in the sunniest spot he could find within hearing.

"Lightfoot's great-great-ever-so-great-grandfather was named Lightfoot too, and was not a whit less handsome than Lightfoot is now," continued Grandfather Frog in his best story-telling voice. "He had just such slim legs as Lightfoot has now and just such wonderful, branching horns. When he had the latter, he was not much afraid of anybody. Those enemies swift enough of foot to catch him he could successfully fight with his horns, and those too big and strong for him to fight were not swift enough to catch him. But there was a season in every year when he had no horns, as is the case with Lightfoot. You know, or ought to know, that every spring Lightfoot loses his horns and through the summer a new pair grows. It was so with Mr. Deer of that long-ago time, and when he lost those great horns, he felt very helpless and timid.

"Now old Mr. Deer loved the open meadows and spent most of his time there. When he had to run, he wanted nothing in the way of his slim legs. And how he could run! My, my, my, how he could run! But there were others who could run swiftly in those days too,—Mr. Wolf and Mr. Dog. Mr. Deer always had a feeling that some day one or the other would catch him. When he had his horns, this thought didn't worry him much, but when he had lost his horns, it worried him a great deal. He felt perfectly helpless then. 'The thing for me to do is to keep out of sight,' said he to himself, and so instead of going out on the meadows and in the open places, he hid among the bushes and in the brush on the edge of the Green Forest and behind the fallen trees in the Green Forest.

"But one thing troubled old Mr. Deer, who wasn't old then, you know. Yes, Sir, one thing troubled him a great deal. He couldn't run fast at all among the bushes and the fallen trees and the old logs. This was a new worry, and it troubled him almost as much as the old worry. He felt that he was in a dreadful fix. You see, hard times had come, and the big and strong were preying on the weak and small in order to live.

"'If I stay out on the meadows, I

cannot fight if I am caught; and if I stay here, I cannot run fast if I am found by my enemies. Oh, dear! Oh, dear! What shall I do?' cried Mr. Deer, as he lay hidden among the branches of a fallen hemlock-tree.

"Just at that very minute along came Mr. Hare, the great - great - ever - so - great - grandfather of your cousin Jumper. A big log was in his path, and he jumped over it as lightly as a feather. Mr. Deer watched him and sighed. If only he could jump like that in proportion to his size, he would just jump over the bushes and the fallen logs and the fallen trees instead of trying to run around them or squeeze between them. Right then he had an idea. Why shouldn't he learn to jump? He could try, anyway. So when he was sure that no one was around to see him, he practised jumping over little low bushes. At first he couldn't do much, but he kept trying and trying, and little by little he jumped higher. It was hard work, and he scraped his slim legs many times when he tried to jump over old logs and stumps.

"Now all this time some one had been watching him, though he didn't know it. It was Old Mother Nature. One day she stopped him as he was trotting along a path. 'What is this you are doing when you think no one is watching?' she demanded, looking very cross. 'Haven't I given you beauty and speed? And yet you are not satisfied!' Mr. Deer hung his head. Then suddenly he threw it up proudly and told Old Mother Nature that he had not complained, but that through his own efforts he was just trying to add to the blessings which he did have, and he explained why he wanted to learn to jump. Old Mother Nature heard him through. 'Let me see you jump over that bush,' she snapped crossly, pointing to a bush almost as high as Mr. Deer himself.

"'Oh, I can't jump nearly as high as that!' he cried. Then tossing his head proudly, he added, 'But I'll try.' So just as Peter Rabbit tried to jump the Laughing Brook when he felt sure that he couldn't, Mr. Deer tried to jump the bush. Just imagine how surprised he was when he sailed over it without even touching the top of it with his hoofs! Old Mother Nature had given him the gift of jumping as a reward for his perseverance and because she saw that he really had need of it.

"So ever since that long-ago day, the Deer have lived where the brush is thickest and the Green Forest most tangled, because they are such great jumpers that they can travel faster there than their enemies, and they are no longer so swift of foot in the open meadows. Now, Peter, let's see you jump over the Laughing Brook."

What do you think Peter did? Why, he tried again, and laughed just as hard as the others when once more he landed in the water with a great splash.

VIII

HOW MR. FLYING SQUIRREL ALMOST GOT WINGS

VIII

HOW MR. FLYING SQUIRREL ALMOST GOT WINGS

JIMMY SKUNK and Peter Rabbit were having a dispute. It was a good-natured dispute, but both Jimmy and Peter are very decided in their opinions, and neither would give in to the other. Finally they decided that as neither could convince the other, they should leave it for Grandfather Frog to decide which was right. So they straightway started for the Smiling Pool, where on his big green lily-pad Grandfather Frog was enjoying the twilight and leading the great Frog chorus. Both agreed that they would accept Grandfather Frog's decision.

You see, each was sure that he was right.

When they reached the Smiling Pool, they found Grandfather Frog looking very comfortable and old and wise. "Good evening, Grandfather Frog. I hope you are feeling just as fine as you look," said Jimmy Skunk, who never forgets to be polite.

"Chug-a-rum! I'm feeling very well, thank you," replied Grandfather Frog. "What brings you to the Smiling Pool this fine evening?" He looked very hard at Peter Rabbit, for he suspected that Peter had come for a story.

"To get the wisest person of whom we know to decide a matter on which Peter and I cannot agree; and who is there so wise as Grandfather Frog?" replied Jimmy.

Grandfather Frog looked immensely

pleased. It always pleases him to be considered wise. "Chug-a-rum!" said he gruffly. "You have a very smooth tongue, Jimmy Skunk. But what is this matter on which you cannot agree?"

"How many animals can fly?" returned Jimmy, by way of answer.

"One," replied Grandfather Frog. "I thought everybody knew that. Flitter the Bat is the only animal who can fly."

"You forget Timmy, the Flying Squirrel!" cried Peter excitedly. "That makes two."

Grandfather Frog shook his head. "Peter, Peter, whatever is the matter with those eyes of yours?" he exclaimed. "They certainly are big enough. I wonder if you ever will learn to use them. Half-seeing is sometimes worse than not seeing at all

Timmy cannot fly any more than I can."

"What did I tell you?" cried Jimmy Skunk triumphantly.

"But I've seen him fly lots of times!" persisted Peter. "I guess that any one who has envied him as often as I have ought to know."

"Hump!" grunted Grandfather Frog. "I guess that's the trouble. There was so much envy that it got into your eyes, and you couldn't see straight. Envy is a bad thing."

Jimmy Skunk chuckled.

"Did you ever see him away from trees?" continued Grandfather Frog.

"No," confessed Peter.

"Did you ever see him cut circles in the air like Flitter the Bat?"

"No-o," replied Peter slowly.

"Of course not," retorted Grandfather Frog. "The reason is because he doesn't fly. He hasn't any wings. What he does do is to coast on the air. He's the greatest jumper and coaster in the Green Forest."

"Coast on the air!" exclaimed Peter. "I never heard of such a thing."

"There are many things you never have heard of," replied Grandfather Frog. "Sit down, Peter, and stop fidgeting, and I'll tell you a story."

The very word story was enough to make Peter forget everything else, and he promptly sat down with his big eyes fixed on Grandfather Frog.

"It happened," began Grandfather Frog, "that way back in the beginning of things, there lived a very timid member of the Squirrel family, own cousin to Mr. Red Squirrel and Mr. Gray Squirrel, but not at all like them, for he was very gentle and very shy. Perhaps this was partly because he was very small and was not big enough or strong enough to fight his way as the others did. In fact, this little Mr. Squirrel was so timid that he preferred to stay out of sight during the day, when so many were abroad. He felt safer in the dusk of evening, and so he used to wait until jolly, round, red Mr. Sun had gone to bed behind the Purple Hills before he ventured out to hunt for his food. Then his quarrelsome cousins had gone to bed, and there was no one to drive him away when he found a feast of good things.

" But even at night there was plenty of danger. There was Mr. Owl to be watched out for, and other night prowlers. In fact, little Mr. Squirrel didn't feel safe on the ground a minute, and so he kept to the trees as much as possible. Of course, when the branches of one tree reached to the branches of another tree, it was an easy matter to travel through the tree-tops, but every once in a while there would be open places to cross, and many a fright did timid little Mr. Squirrel have as he scampered across these open places. He used to sit and watch old Mr. Bat flying about and wish that he had wings. Then he thought how foolish it was to wish for something he hadn't got and couldn't have.

" 'The thing to do,' said little Mr. Squirrel to himself, 'is to make the most of what I have got. Now I am a pretty good jumper, but if I keep jumping, perhaps I can learn to jump better than I do now.'

" So every night Mr. Squirrel used to go off by himself, where he was sure no one would see him, and practise jumping. He would climb an old stump and then jump as far as he could. Then he would do it all over again ever so many times, and after a little he found that he went farther, quite a little farther, than when he began. Then one night he made a discovery. He found that by spreading his arms and legs out just as far as possible and making himself as flat as he could, he could go almost twice as far as he had been able to go before, and he landed a great deal easier. It was like sliding down on the air. It was great fun, and pretty soon he was spending all his spare time doing it.

"One moonlight night, Old Mother Nature happened along and sat down on a log to watch him. Little Mr. Squirrel didn't see her, and when at last she asked him what he was doing, he was so surprised and confused that he could hardly find his tongue. At last he told her that he was trying to learn to jump better that he might better take care of himself. The idea pleased Old Mother Nature. You know she is always pleased when she finds people trying to help themselves.

" 'That's a splendid idea,' said she. 'I'll help you. I'll make you the greatest jumper in the Green Forest.'

" Then she gave to little Mr. Squirrel something almost but not quite like wings. Between his fore legs and hind legs on each side she stretched a piece of skin that folded right down against his body when he was walking or running so as to hardly show and wasn't in the way at all.

" 'Now,' said she, 'climb that tall tree over yonder clear to the top and then jump with all your might for that tree over there across that open place.'

" It was ten times as far as little Mr

Squirrel ever had jumped before, and the tree was so tall that he felt sure that he would break his neck when he struck the ground. He was afraid, very much afraid. But Old Mother Nature had told him to do it. He knew that he ought to trust her. So he climbed the tall tree. It was a frightful distance down to the ground, and that other tree was so far away that it was foolish to even think of reaching it.

"'Jump!' commanded Old Mother Nature.

"Little Mr. Squirrel gulped very hard, trying to swallow his fear. Then he jumped with all his might, and just as he had taught himself to do, spread himself out as flat as he could. Just imagine how surprised he was and how tickled when he just coasted down on the air clear across the open place and landed as lightly as a feather on the foot of that distant tree! You see, the skin between his legs when he spread them out had kept him from falling straight down. Of course if he hadn't jumped with all his might, as Old Mother Nature had told him to, even though he thought it wouldn't be of any use, he wouldn't have reached that other tree.

"He was so delighted that he wanted to do it right over again, but he didn't forget his manners. He first thanked Old Mother Nature.

"She smiled. 'See that you keep out of danger, for that is why I have made you the greatest jumper in the Green Forest,' said she.

"Little Mr. Squirrel did. People who, like Peter, did not use their eyes, thought that he could fly, and he was called the Flying Squirrel. He was the great - great - ever - so - great - grandfather of Timmy whom you both know."

"And Timmy doesn't really fly at all, does he?" asked Jimmy Skunk.

"Certainly not. He jumps and slides on the air," replied Grandfather Frog.

"What did I tell you?" cried Jimmy triumphantly to Peter.

"Well, anyway, it's next thing to flying. I wish I could do it," replied Peter.

IX

HOW MR. WEASEL WAS MADE AN OUTCAST

IX

HOW MR. WEASEL WAS MADE AN OUTCAST

CHATTERER THE RED SQUIRREL peered down from the edge of an old nest built long ago in a big hemlock-tree in the Green Forest, and if you could have looked into Chatterer's eyes, you would have seen there a great fear. He looked this way; he looked that way. Little by little, the fear left him, and when at last he saw Peter Rabbit coming his way, he gave a little sigh of relief and ran down the tree. Peter saw him and headed straight toward him to pass the time of day.

"Peter," whispered Chatterer, as

soon as Peter was near enough to hear, "have you seen Shadow the Weasel?"

It was Peter's turn to look frightened, and he hastily glanced this way and that way. "No," he replied. "Is he anywhere about here?"

"I saw him pass about five minutes ago, but he seemed to be in a hurry, and I guess he has gone now," returned Chatterer, still whispering.

"I hope so! My goodness, I hope so!" exclaimed Peter, still looking this way and that way uneasily.

"I hate him!" declared Chatterer fiercely.

"So do I," replied Peter. "I guess everybody does. It must be dreadful to be hated by everybody. I don't believe he has got a single friend in the wide, wide world, not even among his own relatives. I wonder why it is he never tries to make any friends."

"Here comes Jimmy Skunk. Let's ask him. He ought to know, for he is Shadow's cousin," said Chatterer.

Jimmy came ambling up in his usual lazy way, for you know he never hurries. It seemed to Chatterer and Peter that he was slower than usual. But he got there at last.

"Why is it, Jimmy Skunk, that your cousin, Shadow the Weasel, never tries to make any friends?" cried Chatterer, as soon as Jimmy was near enough.

"I've never asked him, but I suppose it's because he doesn't want them," replied Jimmy.

"But why?" asked Peter.

"I guess it's because he is an outcast," replied Jimmy.

"What is an outcast," demanded Peter.

"Why, somebody with whom nobody else will have anything to do, stupid," replied Jimmy. "I thought everybody knew that."

"But how did it happen that he became an outcast in the first place?" persisted Peter.

"He's always been an outcast, ever since he was born, and I suppose he is used to it," declared Jimmy. "His father was an outcast, and his grandfather, and his great-grandfathers way back to the days when the world was young."

"Tell us about it. Do tell us about it!" begged Peter.

Jimmy smiled good-naturedly. "Well, seeing that I haven't anything else to do just now, I will. Perhaps you fellows may learn something from the story," said he. Then he settled himself comfortably with his back to an old stump and began.

"When old King Bear ruled in the

forest long, long ago, and the great-great-ever-so-great-grandfathers of all of us and of everybody else lived in peace and happiness with each other, slim, trim, spry Mr. Weasel lived with the rest. He was small, just as Shadow is now, and he looked just the same as Shadow does now. He was on the best of terms with all his neighbors, and no one had a word to say against him. In fact, he was rather liked and had quite as many friends as anybody. But all the time he had a mean disposition. He hid it from his neighbors, but he had it just the same. Now mean dispositions are easily hidden when everything is pleasant and there are no worries, and that is the way it was then. No one suspected any one else of meanness, for with plenty to eat and nothing to worry about, there was no cause for meanness.

"With his mean disposition, Mr.

Weasel was also very crafty. Being small and moving so swiftly, he was hard to keep track of. You know how it is with Shadow—now you see him, and now you don't."

Chatterer and Peter nodded. They knew that it is because of this that he is called Shadow.

"Well," continued Jimmy, "it didn't take him long to find that if he were careful, he could go where he pleased, and no one would be the wiser. They say that he used to practise dodging out of sight when he saw any one coming, and after a while he got so that he could disappear right under the very noses of his neighbors. Being so slim, he could go where any of his four-footed neighbors could, and it wasn't long before he knew all about every hole and nook and corner anywhere around. There were no secrets that he didn't find out, and all the time no one suspected him.

"Of course hard times came to Mr. Weasel at last, just as to everybody else, but they didn't worry him much. You see, he knew all about the secret hiding-places in which some of his neighbors had stored away food, so when he was hungry, all he had to do was to help himself. So Mr. Weasel became a thief, and still no one suspected him. Now one bad habit almost always leads to another. Mr. Weasel developed a great fondness for eggs. Our whole family has always had rather a weakness that way."

Jimmy grinned, for he knew that Peter and Chatterer knew that he himself never could pass a fresh egg when he found it.

"One day he found a nest in which were four little baby birds instead of the eggs he had been expecting to find there and, having a mean disposition, he flew into a rage and killed those four little birds. Yes, Sir, that's what he did. He found the taste of young birds very much to his liking, and he began to hunt for more. Then he discovered a nest of young mice, and he found these quite as good as young birds. Then came a great fear upon the littlest people, but not once did they suspect Mr. Weasel. He was very crafty and went and came among them just as always. They suspected only the larger and stronger people of the forest who, because food was getting very scarce, had begun to hunt the smaller people.

"But you know wrongdoing is bound to be found out sooner or later. One day Mr. Rabbit surprised Mr. Weasel making a meal of young mice, and of

"One day Mr. Rabbit surprised Mr. Weasel making a meal of young mice."

course he hurried to tell all his neighbors. Then Mr. Weasel knew that it was no longer of use to pretend that he was what he was not, and he boldly joined the bigger animals in hunting the smaller ones. It makes most people angry to be caught in wrongdoing and it was just that way with Mr. Weasel. He flew into a great rage and vowed that he would kill Mr. Rabbit, and when he couldn't catch Mr. Rabbit, he hunted others of his neighbors until there was no one, not even fierce Mr. Wolf or Mr. Panther or Mr. Lynx, of whom the littlest people were in such fear. You see, they could hide from the big hunters, but they couldn't hide from Mr. Weasel because he knew all their hiding-places, and he was so slim and small that wherever they could go, he could go.

"Now the big people, like Mr. Wolf

and Mr. Panther, killed only for food that they might live, and when they found Mr. Weasel killing more than he could eat, they would have nothing to do with him and even threatened to kill him if they caught him. So pretty soon Mr. Weasel found that he hadn't a friend in the world. This made him more savage than ever, and he hunted and killed just for the pleasure of it. He took pleasure in the fear which he read in the eyes of his neighbors when they saw him.

"Old Mother Nature was terribly shocked when she discovered what was going on, but she found that she could do nothing with Mr. Weasel. He wasn't sorry for what he had done and he wouldn't promise to do better. 'Very well,' said Old Mother Nature, 'from this time on you and your children and your children's children forever and ever shall be outcasts among the people of the Green Forest and the Green Meadows, hated by all, little and big.' And it has been so to this day. Even I am not on speaking terms with Shadow, although he is my own cousin," concluded Jimmy Skunk.

Peter Rabbit shuddered. "Isn't it dreadful not to have a single friend?" he exclaimed. "I would rather have to run for my life twenty times a day than to be hated and feared and without a single friend. I wouldn't be an outcast for all the world."

"There's not the least bit of danger of that for you, Peter," laughed Jimmy Skunk.

X

HOW THE EYES OF OLD MR. OWL BECAME FIXED

X

HOW THE EYES OF OLD MR. OWL BECAME FIXED

BLACKY THE CROW had discovered Hooty the Owl dozing the bright day away in a thick hemlock-tree. Blacky knew that the bright light hurt Hooty's big eyes and half blinded him. This meant that he could have no end of fun teasing Hooty, and that Hooty would have to sit still and take it all, because he couldn't see well enough to fly away or to try to catch Blacky. Now if the day had been dark, as it sometimes is on cloudy days, or if the dusk of evening had been settling over the Green Meadows and the Green Forest, matters would have been very different. Blacky would have taken care, the very greatest care, not to let Hooty know that he was anywhere around. But as it was, here was a splendid chance to spoil Hooty's sleep and to see him grow very, very angry and do it without running any great risk.

"Caw, caw, caw, caw, caw!" yelled Blacky at the top of his voice, and at once all his relatives came flocking over to join in the fun. Dear me, dear me, such a racket as there was then! They flew over his head, and they settled in the tree all around him, all yelling as hard as ever they could. Everybody within hearing knew what it meant, and everybody who dared to hurried over to watch the fun. Somehow most people seem to take pleasure in seeing some one else made uncomfortable, especially if it is some one of whom they stand in fear and who is for the time being helpless.

Most of the little meadow and forest people are very much afraid of Hooty the Owl as soon as it begins to grow dark, for that is when he can see best and does all his hunting. So, though it wasn't at all nice of them, they enjoyed seeing him tormented by Blacky and his relatives. But all the time they took the greatest care to keep out of sight themselves. Peter Rabbit was there. So was Jumper the Hare and Happy Jack the Gray Squirrel and Chatterer the Red Squirrel and Whitefoot the Wood Mouse and Striped Chipmunk and a lot more. Of course, Sammy Jay was there, but Sammy didn't try to keep out of sight. Oh, my, no! He joined right in with the Crows, calling Hooty all sorts of bad names and flying about just out of reach in the most impudent way. You see he knew just how helpless Hooty was.

Hooty was very, very angry. He hissed, and he snapped his bill, and he told his tormentors what he would do to them if he caught them after dark. And all the time he kept turning his head with its great, round, glaring, yellow eyes so as not to give his tormentors a chance to pull out any of his feathers, as the boldest of them tried to do. Now Hooty can turn his head as no one else can. He can turn it so that he looks straight back over his tail, so that his head looks as if it were put on the wrong way. Then he can snap it around in the other direction so quickly that you can hardly see him do it, and sometimes it seems as if he turned his head clear around.

That interested Peter Rabbit immensely. He couldn't think of anything else. He kept trying to do the same thing himself, but of course he couldn't. He could turn his head sideways, but that was all. He puzzled over it all the rest of the day, and that night, when his cousin, Jumper the Hare, called at the dear Old Briar-patch, the first thing he did was to ask a question.

"Cousin Jumper, do you know why it is that Hooty the Owl can turn his head way around, and nobody else can?"

"Of course I know," replied Jumper. "I thought everybody knew that. It's because his eyes are fixed in their sockets, and he can't turn them. So he turns his whole head in order to see in all directions. The rest of us can roll our eyes, but Hooty can't."

Peter scratched his long left ear with his long right hindfoot, a way he has when he is thinking or is puzzled.

"That's funny," said he. "I wonder why his eyes are fixed."

"Because his great-great-ever-so-great-grandfather rolled his eyes too much," replied Jumper, yawning. "He saw too much. It's a bad thing to see too much."

"Tell me about it. Please do, Cousin Jumper," begged Peter.

Jumper looked up at the moon to see what time of night it was.

"All right," said he, settling himself comfortably. "All the Owl family, way back to the very beginning, have had very big eyes. Old Mr. Owl had them. He could move them just as we can ours. And because they were so big, and because he could roll them, there was very little going on that Mr. Owl didn't see. It happened one day that Old Mother Nature took it into her wise old head to put the little people of the

Green Meadows and the Green Forest to a test. She wanted to see just how many of them she could trust to obey her orders. So she lined them all up in a row. Then she made them turn so that their backs were to her.

"'Now,' said she, 'everybody is to keep eyes to the front. I am going to be very busy back here for a few minutes, but not one of you is to peek. I shall know if you do, and I shall see to it that you never forget it as long as you live.'

"That sounded as if something dreadful might happen, so everybody sat perfectly still looking straight before them. Some of them felt as if they would die of curiosity to know what Old Mother Nature was doing, but for a while no one thought of disobeying. Old Mr. Rabbit just itched all over with curiosity. It seemed to him that he just must turn his head. But for once he managed to get the best of his curiosity and stared straight ahead.

"Now Mr. Owl had tremendous great ears, just as Hooty has to-day. You can't see them because the feathers cover them, but they are there just the same."

Peter nodded. He knew all about those wonderful ears and how they heard the teeniest, weeniest noise when Hooty was flying at night.

"Those big ears," continued Jumper, "heard every little sound that Old Mother Nature made, and they sounded queer to Mr. Owl. 'If I roll back my eyes without turning my head, I believe I can see what she is doing, and she won't be any the wiser,' thought he. So he rolled his eyes back and then looked straight ahead again. What he had seen made him want to see more. He tried it again. Just imagine how he felt when he found that his eyes wouldn't roll. He couldn't move them a bit. All he could do was to stare straight ahead. It frightened him dreadfully, and he kept trying and trying to roll his eyes, but they were fixed fast. He could see in only one direction, the way his head was turned.

"When at last Old Mother Nature told all the little people that they might look, Mr. Owl didn't want to look. He didn't want to face Old Mother Nature, for he knew perfectly well what had happened to his eyes. He knew that Old Mother Nature had seen him roll them back, and that as a punishment she had fixed them so that he would always stare straight ahead. He didn't say anything. He was too ashamed to. He flew away home the very first chance he got. For a long time after that, Mr. Owl never could see behind him at all. He could only turn his head part way, the same as most folks, and he couldn't roll his eyes to see the rest of the way. It made him dreadfully nervous and unhappy. He felt all the time as if people were doing things behind his back. But he didn't complain. He was ashamed to do that.

"Old Mother Nature was watching him all the time. After a long, long while, she decided that he had been punished enough. But she didn't want him to forget, so she kept his eyes fixed so that they would look straight ahead; but she gave him the power to turn his head farther than any one else, so that he could look straight behind him without turning his body at all. And ever since that time, all Owls have had fixed eyes, but have been able to turn their heads so as to make them look as if they were facing the wrong way."

"Thank you, Cousin Jumper," cried Peter. "But there is one thing you forgot to tell. What was it that Old Mother Nature was doing when Mr. Owl rolled his eyes to look back."

"That," replied Jumper, "Mr. Owl never told, and nobody else knew, so I can't tell you."

XI

HOW IT HAPPENS JOHNNY CHUCK SLEEPS ALL WINTER

XI

HOW IT HAPPENS JOHNNY CHUCK SLEEPS ALL WINTER

PETER RABBIT was bothered. He was bothered in his mind, and when Peter is bothered in his mind, he loses his appetite. It was so now. He had been up in the Old Orchard and, as is his way, had stopped at Johnny Chuck's for a bit of gossip. As he sat there talking, it suddenly came over him that Johnny was looking unusually fat. He said so. Johnny yawned in a very sleepy way as he replied:

"One has to get fat in order to sleep comfortably all winter. I've got to get fatter than I am now before I turn in."

And with that, Johnny Chuck fell to eating as if his sides were falling in instead of threatening to burst, and Peter could get no more from him.

So he went home to think it over, and the more he thought, the more troubled he became. How could anybody sleep all winter? And what good did just getting fat do? Johnny Chuck couldn't eat his own fat, so what was the use of it? "Must be it's to keep him warm," thought Peter and brightened up. But why wasn't a good thick coat of fur just as good or even better? He didn't have any trouble keeping warm. Neither did Billy Mink or Little Joe Otter or Reddy Fox. No, it couldn't be that Johnny Chuck put on all that fat just to keep warm. Besides, he would spend the winter way down deep in the ground, and there was no excuse for being cold there.

"I couldn't sleep all winter if I wanted to, and I wouldn't if I could, for there is too much fun to miss," muttered Peter, as he started for the Smiling Pool in search of Grandfather Frog. He found him sitting on his big lily-pad, but somehow Grandfather Frog didn't look as chipper and smart as usual. "He certainly is growing old," thought Peter. "He isn't as spry as he used to be. Seems as if he had grown old in the last two or three weeks. Too bad, too bad."

Aloud, Peter said: "Why, Grandfather Frog, how well you are looking! You are enough to make us young fellows envious."

Grandfather Frog looked at Peter sharply. Perhaps he read the truth in Peter's eyes. "Chug-a-rum!" said he. "Be honest, Peter. Be honest. Don't try to flatter, because it is a bad habit to get into. I know how I look. I look old and tired. Now isn't that so?"

Peter looked a little shamefaced. He didn't know just what to say, so he said nothing and just nodded his head.

"That's better," said Grandfather Frog gruffly. "Always tell the truth. The fact is I *am* tired. I am so tired that I'm going to sleep for the winter, and I'm going to do it this very day."

"Oh, Grandfather Frog," (Peter had found his tongue), "please tell me something before you go. I can understand how you may want to sleep all winter because you have no nice fur coat to keep you warm, but why does Johnny Chuck do it, and how does he do it? Why doesn't he starve to death?"

Grandfather Frog had to smile at the eager curiosity in Peter's voice. "I see you are just as full of questions as ever, Peter," said he. "I suppose I may as well tell you one more story, because it will be a long time before you will get another from me. Johnny Chuck sleeps all winter because he is sensible, and he is sensible because it runs in the family to be sensible. His great - great - ever - so - great - grandfather was sensible. It's a very good thing to have good sound common sense run in the family, Peter."

Once more Peter nodded his head. Jerry Muskrat, who was sitting on the Big Rock, listening, winked at Peter, and Peter winked back. Then he made himself comfortable and prepared not to miss a word of Grandfather Frog's story.

"You must know, Peter, that a long time ago when the world was young, there was a time when there was no winter," began Grandfather Frog

"That was before the hard times of which I have told you before. Everybody had plenty to eat, and everybody was on the best of terms with all his neighbors. Then came the hard times, and the beginning of the hard times was the coming of rough Brother North Wind and Jack Frost. Their coming made the first winter. It wasn't a very long or a very hard winter, but it was long enough and hard enough to make a great deal of discomfort, particularly for those little people who lived altogether on tender young green plants. Yes, Sir, it certainly was hard on them. Some of them nearly starved to death that first winter, short as it was. Old Mr. Chuck, who, of course, wasn't old then, was one of them. By the time the tender, young, green things began to grow again, he was just a shadow of what he used to be. He was so thin that sometimes he used to listen to see if he couldn't hear his bones rattle inside his skin.

"Of course he couldn't, but he was quite sure that when the wind blew, it went right through him. At last warm weather returned, just as it does now every summer, and once more there was plenty to eat. Some of the little people seemed to forget all about the hard times of the cold weather, but not Mr. Chuck. He had been too cold and too hungry to ever forget. Of course, with plenty to eat, he soon grew fat and comfortable again, but all the time he kept thinking about the terrible visit of rough Brother North Wind and Jack Frost and wondering if they would come again. He talked about it with his neighbors but most of them laughed and told him that he was borrowing trouble, and that they didn't believe that Brother North Wind and Jack Frost ever would come again.

"So after a while Mr. Chuck kept his thoughts to himself and went about his business as usual. But all the time he was turning over and over in his mind the possibility of another period of cold and starvation and trying to think of some way to prepare for it. He didn't once think of going to Old Mother Nature and begging her to take care of him, for he was very independent, was Mr. Chuck, and believed that those are best helped who help themselves. So he kept studying and studying how he could live through another cold spell, if it should come.

"'I haven't got as thick a fur coat as Mr. Mink or Mr. Otter or Mr. Squirrel or some others, and I can't run around as fast as they can, so of course I can't keep as warm,' said he to himself, as he sat taking a sun-bath one day. 'I must find some other way of keeping warm. Now I don't believe the cold can get very deep down in the ground, so if I build me a house way down deep in the ground, it always will be comfortable. Anyway, it never will be very cold. I believe that is a good idea. I'll try it at once.'

"So without wasting any time, Mr. Chuck began to dig. He dug and he dug and he dug. When his neighbors grew curious and asked questions, he smiled good-naturedly and said that he was trying an experiment. When he had made a long hall which went down so deep that he was quite sure that Jack Frost could not get down there, he made a bedroom and put in it a bed of soft grass. When it was finished, he was so pleased with it that he retired to it every night as soon as the sun went down and didn't come out again until morning.

"'Anyway, I won't freeze to death,' said he. Then he sighed as he remembered how hungry, how terribly hungry he had been. 'Now if only I can think of some way to get food enough to carry me through, I'll be all right.'

"At first he thought of storing up food, but when he tried that, he soon found that the tender green things on which he lived wouldn't keep. They shriveled and dried, so that he couldn't eat them at all. He was still trying to think of some plan when Old Mother Nature sent warning that rough Brother North Wind and Jack Frost were coming again. Mr. Chuck's heart sank. He thought of how soon all the tender green things would disappear. Right then an idea was born in Mr. Chuck's head. He would eat all he could while he could, and then he would go down into his bedroom and sleep just as long as he could!

"So day after day he spent stuffing himself, and his neighbors called him Mr. Greedy. But he didn't mind that. He kept right on eating, and of course he grew fatter and fatter, so that at last he was so fat he could hardly get about. The days grew cooler and cooler, and then Mr. Chuck noticed that because he was so fat, he didn't feel the cold as he had before. There came a morning at last when Mr. Chuck stuck his nose out to find Jack Frost waiting to pinch it. All the tender green things were black and dead. Back to his bed scrambled Mr. Chuck and curled up to sleep just as long as he could. He made up his mind that he wouldn't worry until he had to. He had done his best, and that was all he could do.

"When Old Mother Nature came to see how the little people were faring, she missed Mr. Chuck. She asked his neighbors what had become of him, but no one knew. At length she came to his house and looking inside found him fast asleep. She saw right away what he had done and how fat he had grown. She knew without being told what it all meant, and the idea amused her. Instead of wakening him, as she had at first intended to do, she touched Mr. Chuck and put him into a deeper sleep, saying:

"'You shall sleep, Mr. Chuck,
Through the time of frost and snow.
For your courage and your pluck
You shall no discomfort know.'

"And so Mr. Chuck slept on until the tender young green things began once more to grow. The cold could not reach him, and the fat he had stored under his skin took the place of food. When he awoke in the spring, he knew nothing of the hard times his neighbors were talking about. And ever since then the Chuck family has slept through the winter, because it is the most comfortable and sensible thing to do. I know, because I have done the same thing for years. Good-by, Peter Rabbit! No more stories until spring."

Before Peter could say a word, there was a splash in the Smiling Pool, and Grandfather Frog was nowhere to be seen.

"I—I don't see how they do it," said Peter, shaking his head in a puzzled way as he slowly hopped towards the dear Old Briar-patch.

XII

HOW OLD MR. OTTER LEARNED TO SLIDE

XII

HOW OLD MR. OTTER LEARNED TO SLIDE

LITTLE JOE OTTER was having the jolliest kind of a time. Little Joe Otter is a jolly little chap, anyway, and just now he was extra happy. You see, he had a brand new slippery-slide. Yes, Sir, Little Joe had just built a new slippery-slide down the steepest part of the bank into the Smiling Pool. It was longer and smoother than his old slippery-slide, and it seemed to Little Joe as if he could slide and slide all day long. Of course he enjoyed it more because he had built it himself. He would stretch out full length at the top of the slippery-slide, give a kick to start himself, shoot down the slippery-slide, disappear headfirst with a great splash into the Smiling Pool, and then climb up the bank and do it all over again.

Peter Rabbit and Johnny Chuck sat watching him from the bank on the other side of the Smiling Pool. Right down below them, sitting on his big green lily-pad, was Grandfather Frog, and there was a sparkle in his big, goggly eyes and his great mouth was stretched in a broad grin as he watched Little Joe Otter. He even let a foolish green fly brush the tip of his nose and didn't snap at it.

"Chug-a-rum!" exclaimed Grandfather Frog to no one in particular. "That reminds me of the days when I was young and the greatest diver in the Smiling Pool. My goodness, it makes me feel young just to watch Little Joe shoot down that slippery-slide. If I weren't so old, I'd try it myself. Wheee!"

With that, Grandfather Frog suddenly jumped. It was a great, long, beautiful jump, and with his long hind legs straight out behind him, Grandfather Frog disappeared in the Smiling Pool so neatly that he made hardly a splash at all, only a whole lot of rings on the surface of the water that grew bigger and bigger until they met the rings made by Little Joe Otter and then became all mixed up.

Half a minute later Grandfather Frog's head bobbed up out of the water, and for the first time he saw Johnny Chuck and Peter Rabbit.

"Come on in; the water's fine!" he cried, and rolled one big, goggly eye up at jolly, round, bright Mr. Sun and winked it in the most comical way, for he knew, and he knew that Mr. Sun knew, just how Johnny Chuck and Peter Rabbit dislike the water.

"No, thanks," replied Peter, but there was a wistful look in his big eyes as he watched Little Joe Otter splash into the Smiling Pool. Little Joe was having such a good time! Peter actually was wishing that he *did* like the water.

Grandfather Frog climbed out on his big green lily-pad. He settled himself comfortably so as to face Johnny Chuck and Peter and at the same time watch Little Joe out of the corner of one big, goggly eye.

"Chug-a-rum!" said he, as once more Little Joe splashed into the Smiling Pool. "Did you ever hear about Little Joe's family secret?" he asked in his deep gruff voice.

"No," cried Peter Rabbit. "Do tell us about it! I just love secrets."

There was a great deal of eagerness in Peter's voice, and it made Grandfather Frog smile.

"Is that the reason you never can keep them?" he asked.

Peter looked a wee bit foolish, but he kept still and waited patiently. After what seemed a long, long time, Grandfather Frog cleared his throat two or three times, and this is the story he told Johnny Chuck and Peter Rabbit:

"Once upon a time when the world was young, the great-great-ever-so-great-grandfather of Little Joe Otter got into a peck of trouble. Yes, Sir, he certainly did get into a peck of trouble. You see, it was winter, and everything was covered with snow, so that food was hard to get. Most of the little forest and meadow people found little to eat, and it took a great deal of hunting to find that little. Only those who, like old Mr. Squirrel, had been wise enough to lay up a store of food when there was plenty, and two or three others like Mr. Mink and Mr. Otter, who could go fishing in the spring-holes which had not frozen over, had full stomachs.

"Now an empty stomach almost always makes a short temper. It is hard, very hard indeed to be hungry and good-natured at the same time. So as most of the people of the Green Forest were hungry all the time, they were also short-tempered all the time. Mr. Otter knew this. When any of them came prowling around the spring-hole where he was fishing, he would tease them by letting them see how fat he was. Sometimes he would bring up a fine fish and eat it right before them without offering to share so much as a mouthful. He had done this several times to Mr. Lynx, and though Mr. Lynx had begged and begged for just a bite, Mr. Otter had refused the teeniest, weeniest bit and had even made fun of Mr. Lynx for not being smart enough to get sufficient to eat.

"Now it happened that one fine morning Mr. Otter took it into his head to take a walk in the Green Forest. It was a beautiful morning, and Mr. Otter went farther than he intended. He was just trying to make up his mind whether to turn back or go just a little farther, when he heard stealthy footsteps behind him. He looked over his shoulder, and what he saw helped him to make up his mind in a hurry. There, creeping over the frozen snow, was Mr. Lynx, and the sides of Mr. Lynx were very thin, and the eyes of Mr. Lynx looked very hungry and fierce, and the claws of Mr. Lynx were very long and strong and cruel looking. Mr. Otter made up his mind right away that the cold, black water of that open spring-hole was the only place for him, and he started for it without even passing the time of day with Mr. Lynx.

"Now Mr. Otter's legs were very short, just as Little Joe's are, but it was surprising how fast he got over the snow that beautiful morning. When he came to the top of a little hill, he would slide down, because he found that he could go faster that way. But in spite of all he could do, Mr. Lynx traveled faster, coming with great jumps and snarling and spitting with every jump. Mr. Otter was almost out of breath when he reached the high bank just above the open spring-hole. It was very steep, very steep indeed. Mr. Otter threw a hasty glance over his shoulder. Mr. Lynx was so near that in one more jump he would catch him.

There wasn't time to run around to the place where the bank was low. Mr. Otter threw himself flat, gave a frantic kick with his hind legs, shut his eyes, and shot down, down, down the slippery bank so fast that he lost what little breath he had left. Then he landed with a great splash in the cold, black water and was safe, for Mr. Lynx was afraid of the water. He stopped right on the very edge of the steep bank, where he growled and screeched and told Mr. Otter what dreadful things he would do to him if ever he caught him.

"Now in spite of his dreadful fright, Mr. Otter had enjoyed that exciting slide down the steep bank. He got to thinking about it after Mr. Lynx had slunk away into the Green Forest, and when he was rested and could breathe comfortably again, he made up his mind to try it once more. So he climbed out where the bank was low and ran around to the steep place and once more slid down into the water. It was great fun, the greatest fun Mr. Otter ever had had. He did it again and again. In fact, he kept doing it all the rest of that day. And he found that the more he slid, the smoother and more slippery became the slippery-slide, for the water dripped from his brown coat and froze on the slide.

"After that, as long as the snow lasted, Mr. Otter spent all his time, between eating and sleeping, sliding down his slippery-slide. He learned just how to hold his legs so that they would not be hurt. When gentle Sister South Wind came in the spring and took away all the snow, Mr. Otter hardly knew what to do with himself, until one day a bright idea popped into his head and made him laugh aloud. Why not make a slippery-slide of mud and clay? Right away he tried it. It wasn't as good as the snow slide, but by trying and trying, he found a way to make it better than at first. After that Mr. Otter was perfectly happy, for summer and winter he had a slippery-slide. He taught his children, and they taught their children how to make slippery-slides, and ever since that long-ago day when the world was young, the making of slippery-slides has been the family secret of the Otters."

"And it's the best secret in the world," said Little Joe Otter, swimming up behind Grandfather Frog just then.

"I wish—I wish I had a slippery-slide," said Peter Rabbit wistfully.

"Chug-a-rum!" said Grandfather Frog. "Chug-a-rum! Be content with the blessings you have got, Peter Rabbit. Be content with the blessings you have got. No good comes of wishing for things which it never was meant that you should have. It is a bad habit and it makes discontent."

XIII

HOW DRUMMER THE WOODPECKER CAME BY HIS RED CAP

XIII

HOW DRUMMER THE WOODPECKER CAME BY HIS RED CAP

DRUMMER THE WOODPECKER was beating his long roll on a hollow tree in the Green Forest. Rat-a-tat-tat-tat-tat! Rat-a-tat-tat-tat-tat! Drummer thought it the most beautiful sound in the world. After each long roll he would stop and listen for a reply. You see, sometimes one of his family in another part of the Green Forest, or over in the Old Orchard, would hear him drumming and would hasten to find a hollow tree himself and drum too. Then they would drum back and forth to each other for the longest time, until all the other little people would scold because of the racket and would wish they could stop their ears. But it was music, real music to Drummer and all the members of his family, and Drummer never was happier than when beating his long roll as he was doing now.

Rat-a-tat-tat-tat! Rat-a-tat-tat-tat! Suddenly Drummer heard a scratching sound inside the hollow tree. Once more he beat the long roll and the scratching sound grew louder. Then he heard a voice just a little way above him.

"Do Ah hear some one knocking?" asked the voice.

Drummer looked up. There was Unc' Billy Possum's sharp little face sticking out of his doorway, and Unc' Billy looked very sleepy and very cross and at the same time as if he were trying very hard to be polite and pleasant.

"Hello, Unc' Billy! Is this your house? I didn't know it when I began to drum. I wasn't knocking; I was drumming. I just love to drum," replied Drummer.

"Ah reckons yo' do by the noise yo' have been making, but Ah don't like being inside the drum. Ah'm feelin' powerful bad in the haid just now, Brer Drummer, and Ah cert'nly will take it kindly if yo' will find another drum," said Unc' Billy, holding his head in both hands as if he had a terrible headache.

Drummer looked disappointed and a little bit hurt, but he is one of the best-natured little people in the Green Forest and always willing to be obliging.

"I'm sorry if I have disturbed you, Unc' Billy," he replied promptly. "Of course I won't drum here any longer, if you don't like it. I'll look for another hollow tree, though I don't believe I can find another as good. It is one of the best sounding trees I have ever drummed on. It's simply beautiful!" There was a great deal of regret in his voice, as if it were the hardest work to give up that tree.

"Ah'll tell yo' where there's another just as good," replied Unc' Billy. "Yo' see the top of that ol' chestnut-tree way down there in the holler? Well, yo' try that. Ah'm sure yo' will like it."

Drummer thanked Unc' Billy politely and bobbed his red-capped head as he spread his wings and started in the direction of the big chestnut-tree. Unc' Billy grinned as he watched him. Then he slowly and solemnly winked one eye at Peter Rabbit, who had just come along.

"What's the joke?" asked Peter.

"Ah done just sent Brer Drummer down to the big chestnut-tree to drum," Unc' Billy replied, winking again.

"Why, that's Bobby Coon's house!" cried Peter, and then he saw the joke and began to grin too.

In a few minutes they heard Drummer's long roll. Then again and again. The third time it broke off right in the middle, and right away a terrible fuss started down at the big chestnut-tree. They could hear Drummer's voice, and it sounded very angry.

"Ah reckon Brer Coon was waked up and lost his temper," chuckled Unc' Billy. "It's a bad habit to lose one's temper. Yes, Sah, it cert'nly is a bad habit. Ah reckons Ah better be turning in fo' another nap, Brer Rabbit." With that Unc' Billy disappeared, still chuckling.

Hardly was he out of sight when

Peter saw Drummer heading that way, and Drummer looked very much put out about something. He just nodded to Peter and flew straight to Unc' Billy's tree. Then he began to drum. How he did drum! His red-capped head flew back and forth as Peter never had seen it fly before. Rat-a-tat-tat-tat-tat! Rat-a-tat-tat-tat! Rat-a-tat-tat-tat-tat! Drummer hardly paused for breath. There was too much noise for Peter, and he kicked up his heels and started for the Smiling Pool, and all the way there he laughed.

"I hope Unc' Billy is enjoying a good nap," he chuckled. "Drummer certainly has turned the joke back on Unc' Billy this time, and I guess it serves him right."

He was still laughing when he reached the Smiling Pool. Grandfather Frog watched him until he began to smile too. You know laughter is catching. "Ha, ha, ha! Ho, ho, ho!" laughed Peter and held his sides.

"What is the joke?" demanded Grandfather Frog in his deepest voice.

When Peter could get his breath, he told Grandfather Frog all about the joke on Unc' Billy Possum. "Listen!" said Peter at the end of the story. They both listened. Rat-a-tat-tat-tat-tat! The long roll of Drummer the Woodpecker could be heard clear down to the Smiling Pool, and Peter and Grandfather Frog knew by the sound that it still came from Unc' Billy's house.

"Chug-a-rum! That reminds me," said Grandfather Frog. "Did you ever hear how Drummer came by his red cap?"

"No," replied Peter. "How did he?" There was great eagerness in Peter's voice.

"Well," said Grandfather Frog, settling himself in a way that Peter knew meant a story, "of course Drummer over there came by his red cap because it was handed down in the family, but of course there's a reason."

"Of course," said Peter, quite as if he knew all about it.

Grandfather Frog rolled his great, goggly eyes and looked at Peter suspiciously, but Peter looked so innocent and eager that he went on with his story.

"Of course, it all happened way back in the days when the world was young."

"Of course!" said Peter.

This time Grandfather Frog took no notice. "Drummer's grandfather a thousand times removed was just a plain little black and white bird without the least bit of bright color on him.

He didn't have any sweeter voice than Drummer has to-day. Altogether he seemed to his neighbors a no-account little fellow, and they didn't have much to do with him. So Mr. Woodpecker lived pretty much alone. In fact, he lived alone so much that when he found a hollow tree he used to pound on it just to make a noise and keep from being lonesome, and that is how he learned to drum. You see, he hadn't any voice for singing, and so he got in the habit of drumming to keep his spirits up.

"Now all the time, right down in his heart, Mr. Woodpecker envied the birds who had handsome coats. He used to wish and wish that he had something bright, if it were no more than a pretty necktie. But he never said anything about it, and no one suspected it but Old Mother Nature, and Mr. Woodpecker didn't know that she knew it.

Whenever he got to wishing too much, he would try to forget it by hunting for worms that bored into the trees of the Green Forest and which other birds could not get because they did not have the stout bill and the long tongue Mr. Woodpecker possessed.

"Now it happened that while Old Mother Nature was busy elsewhere, a great number of worms settled in the Green Forest and began to bore into the trees, so that after a while many trees grew sickly and then died. None of the other little people seemed to notice it, or if they did, they said it was none of their business and that Old Mother Nature ought to look out for such things. They shrugged their shoulders and went on playing and having a good time. But Mr. Woodpecker was worried. He loved the Green Forest dearly, and he began to fear that if something wasn't done, there wouldn't be any Green Forest. He said as much to some of his neighbors, but they only laughed at him. The more he thought about it, the more Mr. Woodpecker worried.

"'Something must be done,' said he to himself. 'Yes, Sir, something must be done. If Old Mother Nature doesn't come to attend to things pretty soon, it will be too late.' Then he made up his mind that he would do what he could. From early morning until night he hunted worms and dug them out of the trees. He would start at the bottom of a tree and work up, going all over it until he was sure that there wasn't another worm left. Then he would fly to the next tree. He pounded with his bill until his neck ached. He didn't even take time to drum. His neighbors laughed at him at first, but he kept right on working, working, working every hour of the day.

"At last Old Mother Nature appeared very unexpectedly. She went all through the Green Forest, and her sharp eyes saw all that Mr. Woodpecker had done. She didn't say a word to him, but she called all the little people of the Green Forest before her, and when they were all gathered around, she sent for Mr. Woodpecker. She made him sit up on a dead limb of a tall chestnut-tree where all could see him. Then she told just what he had done, and how he had saved the Green Forest, and how great a debt the other little people owed to him.

"'And now that you may never forget it,' she concluded, 'I herewith make Mr. Woodpecker the policeman of the trees, and this is his reward to be worn by him and his children forever and ever.' With that she called Mr. Woodpecker down before her and put on his head a beautiful red cap, for she knew how in his heart he had longed to wear something bright. Mr. Woodpecker thanked Old Mother Nature as best he could and then slipped away where he could be alone with his happiness. All the rest of the day the other little people heard him drumming off by himself in the Green Forest and smiled, for they knew that that was the way he was expressing his joy, having no voice to sing.

"And that," concluded Grandfather Frog, "is how Drummer whom you know came by his red cap."

"Isn't it splendid!" cried Peter Rabbit, and then he and Grandfather Frog both smiled as they heard a long rat-a-tat-tat-tat roll out from the Green Forest.

XIV

HOW OLD MR. TREE TOAD FOUND OUT HOW TO CLIMB

XIV

HOW OLD MR. TREE TOAD FOUND OUT HOW TO CLIMB

OF all the puzzling things over which Peter Rabbit had sat and thought and wondered until the brains in that funny little head of his were topsy-turvy, none was more puzzling than the fact that Sticky-toes the Tree Toad could climb. Often Peter had watched him climb up the trunk of a tree or jump from one branch to another and then thought of Old Mr. Toad, own cousin to Sticky-toes, and of Grandfather Frog, another own cousin, who couldn't climb at all, and wondered how it had all come about that one cousin could climb and be just as much at home in the trees as the birds, while the others couldn't climb at all.

He had it on his mind one morning when he met Old Mr. Toad solemnly hopping down the Lone Little Path. Right then and there Peter resolved to ask Old Mr. Toad. "Good morning, Mr. Toad," said Peter politely. "Have you a few minutes to spare?"

Old Mr. Toad hopped into the shade of a big mullein leaf. "I guess so, if it is anything important," said he. "Phew! Hot, isn't it? I simply can't stand the sun. Now what is that you've got on your mind, Peter?"

Peter hesitated a minute, for he wasn't at all sure that Old Mr. Toad would think the matter sufficiently important for him to spend his time in story telling. Then he blurted out the whole matter and how he had puzzled and puzzled why Sticky-toes was able to climb when none of the rest of the Toad family could. Old Mr. Toad chuckled.

"Looking for a story as usual, I see," said he. "You ought to go to Grandfather Frog for this one, because Sticky-toes is really a Frog and not a Toad. But we are all cousins, and I don't mind telling you about Sticky-toes, or rather about his great-great-ever-so-great-grandfather, who was the first of the family ever to climb a tree. You see, it is all in the family, and I am very proud of my family, which is one of the very oldest."

Peter settled himself comfortably and prepared to listen. Old Mr. Toad snapped up a foolish spider who came too near and then cleared his throat.

"Once on a time," he began, "when Old Mother Nature made the first land and the first trees and plants, the Toads and the Frogs were the first to leave the water to see what dry land was like. The Toads, being bolder than the Frogs, went all over the new land while the Frogs kept within jumping distance of the water, just as Grandfather Frog does to this day. There was one Frog, however, who, seeing how bravely and boldly the Toads went forth to see all that was to be seen in the new land, made up his mind that he too would see the Great World. He was the smallest of the Frogs, and his friends and relatives warned him not to go, saying that he would come to no good end.

"But he wouldn't listen to their dismal croakings and hurried after the Toads. Being able to make longer jumps than they could, he soon caught up with them, and they all journeyed on together. The Toads were so pleased that one of their cousins was brave enough to join them that they made him very welcome and treated him as one of themselves, so that they soon got to thinking of him as a Toad and not as a Frog at all.

"Now the Toads soon found that Old Mother Nature was having a hard time to make plants grow, because as fast as they came up, they were eaten by insects. You see, she had so many things to attend to in those days when the world was young that she had to leave a great many things to take care of themselves and get along the best they could, and it was this way with the plants. It was then that the great idea came to my great-great-ever-so-great-grandfather, and he called all the Toads together and proposed that they help Old Mother Nature by catching the bugs and worms that were destroying the plants.

"Little Mr. Frog, who had been adopted by the Toads, was one of the most eager to help, and he was busy every minute. After a while the Toads had caught most of the bugs and worms on the ground and within reach, and the plants began to grow. But when the plants got above the reach of the Toads, the bugs and the worms were safe once more and began to multiply so that the plants suffered and stopped growing. You see, there were no birds in those days to help. One day little Mr. Frog sat under a bush on which most of the leaves had been eaten. He saw a worm eating a leaf on one of the lower branches. It was quite a way above his head. It worried him. He kept his eyes on that worm and thought and thought until his head ached. At last he got an idea. 'I wonder,' thought he, 'if I jump as hard as I can, if I can catch that fellow. I'll try it. It will do no harm to try.'

"So he drew his long legs close under him, and then he jumped up with all his might. He didn't quite reach the bug, but he got his hands on the branch and by pulling and struggling, he managed to get up on it. It was a very uncertain seat, but he hung on and crept along until he could dart his tongue out and catch that worm. Then he saw another, and in trying to catch that one he lost his balance and fell to the ground with a thump. It quite knocked the wind from his body.

"That night little Mr. Frog studied and studied, trying to think of some way by which he could get up in the bushes and trees and clear them of bugs and worms. 'If only I could hold on once I get up there, I would be all right,' thought he. 'Then I could leave the bugs and worms on the ground for my cousins the Toads to look after, while I look after those beyond their reach.'

"The next day and the next, and for many days thereafter, little Mr. Frog kept jumping for bugs on the bushes. He got many thumps and bumps, but he didn't mind these, for little by little he was learning how to hang on to the branches once he got up in them. Then one day, just by accident, he put one hand against the trunk of a young pine-tree, and when he started to take it away, he found it stuck fast. He had to pull to get it free. Like a flash an idea popped into his head. He rubbed a little of the pitch, for that was what had made his hand stick, on both hands, and then he started to climb a tree. As long as the pitch lasted, he could climb.

"Little Mr. Frog was tickled to death with his discovery, but he didn't say a word to any one about it. Every day he rubbed pitch on his hands and then climbed about in the bushes and low trees, ridding them of bugs and worms. Of course, it wasn't very pleasant to have that pitch on his hands, because dirt and all sorts of things which he happened to touch stuck to them, but he made the best of a bad matter and washed them carefully when he was through with his day's work.

"Quite unexpectedly Old Mother Nature returned to see how the trees and the plants were getting on. You see, she was worried about them. When she found what the Toads had been doing, she was mightily pleased. Then she noticed that some of the bushes and low trees had very few leaves left, while others looked thrifty and strong.

"'That's queer,' said Old Mother Nature to herself and went over to examine a bush. Hanging on to a branch for dear life she saw a queer little fellow who was so busy that he didn't see her at all. It was little Mr. Frog. He was catching bugs as fast as he could. Old Mother Nature wrinkled up her brows. 'Now however did he learn to climb?' thought she. Then she hid where she could watch. By and by she saw little Mr. Frog tumble out of the bush, because, you know, the pitch on his hands had worn off. He hurried over to a pine-tree and rubbed more pitch on and then jumped up into the bush and went to work again.

"You can guess how astonished Old Mother Nature was when she saw this performance. And she was pleased.

Oh, yes, indeed, Old Mother Nature was wonderfully pleased. She was pleased because little Mr. Frog was trying so hard to help her, and she was pleased because he had been so smart in finding a way to climb. When she had laughed until she could laugh no more at the way little Mr. Frog had managed to stick to his work, she took him down very gently and wiped the pitch from his hands. Then she gently pinched the end of each finger and each toe so that they ended in little round discs instead of being pointed as before, and in each little disc was a clean, sticky substance. Then she tossed him up in a tree, and when he touched a branch, he found that he could hold on without the least danger of falling.

"'I appoint you caretaker of my trees,' said Old Mother Nature, and from that day on little Mr. Frog lived in the trees, as did his children and his children's children, even as Sticky-toes does to-day. And though he was really a Frog, he was called the Tree Toad, and the Toads have always been proud to have him so called. And this is the end of the story," concluded Old Mr. Toad.

XV

HOW OLD MR. HERON LEARNED PATIENCE

XV

HOW OLD MR. HERON LEARNED PATIENCE

WHENEVER in the spring or summer Peter Rabbit visited the Smiling Pool or the Laughing Brook, he was pretty sure to run across Longlegs the Heron. The first time Peter saw him, he thought that never in all his life had he seen such a homely fellow. Longlegs was standing with his feet in the water and his head drawn back on his shoulders so that he didn't seem to have any neck at all. Peter sat and stared at him most impolitely. He knew that he was impolite, but for the life of him he couldn't help staring.

"He's all legs," thought Peter. "Old Mother Nature must have been in a hurry when she made his great-great-ever-so-great-grandfather way back when the world was young and forgot to give him a neck. I wonder why he doesn't move."

But Longlegs didn't move. Peter stared as long as his patience held out. Then he gave up and went on to see what else he could find. But in a little while Peter was back again at the place where he had seen Longlegs. He didn't really expect to find him there, but he did. So far as Peter could see, Longlegs hadn't moved. "Must be asleep," thought Peter, and after watching for a few minutes, went away again. Half an hour later Peter was once more back. There stood Longlegs just as before. "Now I *know* he is asleep," muttered Peter.

No sooner were the words out of his mouth than something happened, something so sudden and surprising that Peter lost his balance and nearly fell over backward. The long bill which Peter had seen sticking forth from between those humped-up shoulders darted out and down into the water like a flash. Behind that bill was the longest neck Peter ever had seen! It was so long that Peter blinked to be perfectly sure that his eyes had not been playing him a trick. But they hadn't, for Longlegs was gulping down a little fish he had just caught, and when at last it was down, he stretched his neck up very straight while he looked this way and that way, and Peter just gasped.

"I thought he was all legs, but instead of that he's all neck," muttered Peter.

Then Longlegs slowly drew his head down, and it seemed to Peter as if he must somehow wind that long neck up inside his body to get it so completely out of the way. In a minute Longlegs was standing just as before, with seemingly no neck at all. Peter watched until he grew tired, but Longlegs didn't move again. After that Peter went every chance he had to watch Longlegs, but he never had patience to watch long enough to see Longlegs catch another fish. He spoke of it one day to Grandfather Frog. At the mere mention of Longlegs, Grandfather Frog sat up and took notice.

"Where did you see him?" asked Grandfather Frog, and Peter thought his voice sounded anxious.

"Down the Laughing Brook," replied Peter. "Why?"

"Oh, nothing," said Grandfather

Frog, trying to make his voice sound as if he weren't interested. "I just wondered where the long-legged nuisance might be."

"He's the laziest fellow I ever saw," declared Peter. "He just stands doing nothing all day."

"Huh!" exclaimed Grandfather Frog. "If your family had suffered from him as much as mine has, you would say that he was altogether too busy. Ask the Trout what they think, or the Minnow family."

"Oh," said Peter, "you mean that when he stands still that way he is fishing."

Grandfather Frog nodded.

"Well," said Peter, "all I can say is that he is the most patient fellow I ever saw. I didn't suppose there was such patience."

"He comes rightly by it," returned

Grandfather Frog. "He gets it from his great-great-ever-so-great-grandfather, who lived when the world was young. He learned it then."

"How?" demanded Peter, eager for a story.

Grandfather Frog's eyes took on a far-away look, as if he were seeing into that long-ago past. "Chug-a-rum!" he began. "It always seemed to old Mr. Heron as if Old Mother Nature must have made him last of all the birds and was in such a hurry that she didn't care how he looked. His legs were so long and his neck was so long that all his neighbors laughed at him and made fun of him. He was just as awkward as he looked. His long legs were in his way. He didn't know what to do with his long neck. When he tried to run, everybody shouted with laughter. When he tried to fly, he stretched his

"His legs were so long, and his neck was so long that all his neighbors laughed at him."

long neck out, and then he couldn't keep his balance and just flopped about, while all his neighbors laughed harder than ever. Poor Mr. Heron was ashamed of himself, actually ashamed of himself. He quite overlooked the fact that Old Mother Nature had given him a really beautiful coat of feathers. Some of those who laughed at him would have given anything to have possessed such a beautiful coat. But Mr. Heron didn't know this. He couldn't bear to be laughed at, wherein he was very like most people.

"So he tried his best to keep out of sight as much as possible. Now in those days, as at present, the rushes grew tall beside the Smiling Pool, and among them Mr. Heron found a hiding-place. Because his legs were long, he could wade out in the water and keep quite out of sight of those who lived on the land. So he found a use for his long legs and was glad that they were long. At first he used to go ashore to hunt for food. One day as he was wading ashore, he surprised a school of little fish and managed to catch one. It tasted so good that he wanted more, and every day he went fishing. Whenever he saw little fish swimming where the water was shallow, he would rush in among them and do his best to catch one. Sometimes he did, but more often he didn't. You see, he was so clumsy and awkward that he made a great splashing, and the fish would hear him coming and get away.

"One day after he had tried and tried without catching even one, he stopped just at the edge of the rushes to rest. His long neck ached, and to rest it he laid it back on his shoulders. For a long time he stood there, resting. The water around his feet was cool and comforting. He was very comfortable but for one thing,—he was hungry. He was just making up his mind to go on and hunt for something to eat when he saw a school of little fish swimming straight towards him. 'Perhaps,' thought he, 'if I keep perfectly still, they will come near enough for me to catch one.' So he kept perfectly still. He didn't dare even stretch his long neck up. Sure enough, the little fish swam almost to his very feet. They didn't see him at all. When they were near enough, he darted his long neck forward and caught one without any trouble at all. Mr. Heron was almost as surprised as the fish he had caught. You see, he discovered that with his neck laid back on his shoulders that way, he could dart his head forward ever so much quicker than when he was holding it up straight. It really was a great discovery for Mr. Heron.

"Of course all the other fish darted away in great fright, but Mr. Heron didn't mind. He settled himself in great contentment, for now he was less hungry. By and by some foolish tadpoles came wriggling along. 'I'll just try catching one of them for practice. Maybe they are good to eat,' thought Mr. Heron, and just as before darted his head and great bill downward and caught a tadpole.

"'Um-m, they are good!' exclaimed Mr. Heron, and once more settled himself to watch and wait.

"That was a sad day for the Frog family, but a great day for Mr. Heron when he discovered that tadpoles were good to eat." Grandfather Frog sighed mournfully. "Yes," he continued, "that was a great day for Mr. Heron.

He had discovered that he could gain more by patient waiting than by frantic hunting, and he had found that his long neck really was a blessing. After that, whenever he was hungry, he would stand perfectly still beside some little pool where foolish young fish or careless tadpoles were at play and wait patiently until they came within reach.

"One day he was startled into an attempt to fly by hearing the stealthy footsteps of Mr. Fox behind him. His head was drawn back on his shoulders at the time, and he was so excited that he forgot to straighten it out. Just imagine how surprised he was, and how surprised Mr. Fox was, when he sailed away in beautiful flight, his long legs trailing behind him. With his neck carried that way, he could fly as well as any one. From that day on, no one laughed at Mr. Heron because of his long legs and long neck. Mr. Heron himself became proud of them. You see, he had learned how to use what he had been given. Also he had learned the value of patience. So he was happy and envied no one. But he still liked best to keep by himself and became known as the lone fisherman, just as Longlegs is to-day. Chug-a-rum! Isn't that Longlegs coming this way this very minute? This is no place for me!"

With a great splash Grandfather Frog dived into the Smiling Pool.

XVI

HOW TUFTY THE LYNX HAPPENS TO HAVE A STUMP OF A TAIL

IN all his life Peter Rabbit had seen Tufty the Lynx but once, but that once was enough. Tufty, you know, lives in the Great Woods. But once, when the winter was very cold, he had ventured down into the Green Forest, hoping that it would be easier to get a living there. It was then that Peter had seen him. In fact, Peter had had the narrowest of escapes, and the very memory of it made him shiver. He never would forget that great, gray, skulking form that slipped like a shadow through the trees, that fierce, bearded face, those cruel, pale yellow-green eyes, or that switching stump of a tail.

That tail fascinated Peter. It was just an apology for a tail. For Tufty's size it was hardly as much of a tail as Peter himself has. It made Peter feel a lot better. Also it made him very curious. The first chance he got, he asked his cousin, Jumper the Hare, about it. You know Jumper used to live in the Great Woods where Tufty lives, and Peter felt sure that he must know the reason why Tufty has such a ridiculous stub of a tail. Jumper did know, and this is the story he told Peter:

"Way back in the beginning of things lived old Mr. Lynx."

"I know," interrupted Peter. "He was the great-great-ever-so-great-grandfather of Tufty, and he wasn't old then."

"Who's telling this story?" demanded Jumper crossly. "If you know it why did you ask me?"

"I beg your pardon. Indeed I do. I won't say another word," replied Peter hastily.

"All right, see that you don't. Interruptions always spoil a story," said Jumper. "You are quite right about old Mr. Lynx. He wasn't old then. No one was old, because it was in the beginning of things. At that time Mr. Lynx boasted a long tail, quite as fine a tail as his cousin, Mr. Panther. He was very proud of it. You know there is a saying that pride goes before a fall. It was so with Mr. Lynx. He boasted about his tail. He said that it was the finest tail in the world. He said so much that his neighbors got tired of hearing about it. He made a perfect nuisance of himself. He switched and waved his long tail about continually.

It seemed as if that tail were never still. He made fun of those whose tails were shorter or of different shape or less handsome. He quite forgot that that tail had been given him by Old Mother Nature, but talked and acted as if he had grown that tail himself.

"When at last his neighbors could stand it no longer, they decided to teach him a lesson. One day while he was off hunting, they held a meeting, and it was decided that the very next time that Mr. Lynx boasted of his tail old King Bear should slip up behind him and step on it as close to his body as he could, and then each of the others should pull a little tuft of hair from it, so that it would be a long time before Mr. Lynx would be able to boast of its beauty again.

"The chance came that very evening. Mr. Lynx had had a very successful day, and he was feeling very fine. He began to boast of what a great hunter he was, and of how very clever and very smart he was, and then, as usual, he got to boasting about his tail. He was so intent on his boasting that he didn't notice old King Bear slipping around behind him. Old King Bear waited until that long tail was still for just an instant, and then he stepped on it as close to the roots of it as he could. Then all the other little people shouted with glee and began to pull little tufts of hair from it, until it was the most disreputable-looking tail ever seen.

" Old Mr. Lynx let out a yowl and a screech that was enough to make your blood run cold. But he couldn't do a thing, though he tore the ground up with his great claws and pulled with all his might. You see, old King Bear was very big and very heavy, and Mr. Lynx couldn't budge his tail a bit. And he couldn't turn to fight old King Bear, though it seemed as if he would turn himself inside out trying to.

"At last, when old King Bear thought he had been punished enough, he gave the word to the others, and they all scattered to safe hiding-places, for they were of no mind to be within reach of those great claws of Mr. Lynx. Then old King Bear let him go.

"'By the looks of it, I hardly think that you will boast of that tail for a long time to come, Mr. Lynx,' said he in his deep, rumbly-grumbly voice.

"Mr. Lynx turned and screamed in old King Bear's face, but that was all he dared do, for you know old King Bear was very big and strong. Then he turned and slunk away in the shadows by himself. Now Mr. Lynx had a terrible temper, and when he saw how ragged and disreputable his once beautiful tail looked, he flew into a terrible rage, and he swore that no one should laugh at his tail. What do you think he did?"

"What?" asked Peter eagerly.

"He bit it off," replied Jumper slowly. "Yes, Sir, he bit it off right at the place where old King Bear had stepped on it. Of course he was sorry the minute he had done it, but it was done, and that was all there was to it. After that he kept out of sight of all his neighbors. He prowled around mostly at night and was very stealthy and soft-footed, always keeping in the shadows. His temper grew worse and worse from brooding over his lost tail. When any one chanced to surprise him, he would switch his stub of a tail just as he used to switch his long tail. You see he would forget. Then when he was laughed at by those bigger than he, he would scream angrily and slink away like a great, gray shadow.

"Once he besought Old Mother Nature to give him a new tail, but in vain. She gave him a lecture which he never forgot. She told him that it was no one's fault but his own that he had lost the beautiful tail that he did have and had nothing but a stub left. Mr. Lynx crawled on his stomach to the feet of Old Mother Nature and begged with tears in his eyes. Old Mother Nature looked him straight in the eyes, but he couldn't look straight back. He tried, but he couldn't do it. He would shift his eyes from side to side.

"'Look me straight in the face, Mr. Lynx, and tell me that if I give you a handsome new tail, you will never boast about it or take undue pride in it,' said she.

"Mr. Lynx looked her straight in the face and said 'I—' Then his eyes shifted. He brought them back to Old Mother Nature's face with a jerk and began again. 'I promise—' Once more his eyes shifted. Then he gave up and sneaked away into the darkest shadows he could find. You see, he couldn't look Old Mother Nature in the face and tell a lie, and that was just what he had been trying to do. The only reason he wanted a new tail was so that he could be proud of it and boast of it as he had of the old one. He hadn't a single real use for it, as he had found out since he had had only that stub.

"Old Mother Nature knew this perfectly well, for you can't fool her, and it's of no use to try. So Mr. Lynx never did get a new tail. He continued to live very much by himself in the darkest parts of the Green Forest, never showing himself to others if he could help it. To the little people, he was like a fearsome shadow to be watched out for at all times. His children were just like him, and his children's children. Tufty is the same way. No one likes him. All who are smaller than he fear him. And if he knows why he has only a stub of a tail, he never mentions it. But you will notice that he switches it just as if it were a real tail. I think he likes to imagine that it is a real one."

"I've noticed," replied Peter. He was silent for a few minutes. Then he added: "Isn't it curious how often we want things we don't need at all, and how those are the things that make us the most trouble in this world?"

THE END